Daisy Rodriguez

The PRINCE *Within*

THE DESCENT TO HELL

Daisy Rodriguez

THE DESCENT TO HELL

CITIOFBOOKS, INC.
3736 Eubank NE Suite A1
Albuquerque, NM 87111-3579
www.citiofbooks.com
Hotline: 1 (877) 389-2759
Fax: 1 (505) 930-7244

Ordering Information:
Quantity sales. Special discounts are available on quantity purchases by corporations, associations, and others. For details, contact the publisher at the address above.

Printed in the United States of America.

ISBN-13:   Softcover   979-8-89391-922-6
                     eBook   979-8-89391-923-3

Library of Congress Control Number: 2025919654

Table of Contents

Chapter One

A year has passed since my epic failed fight with Zozo. That summer after the fight it was rough for me. Mentally I had to get use to my grandfather's body being used by a demon. My half possession with Mammon and finding out I have angelic powers. I have been so blessed not to have gone through this alone, my aunt, Jason and Robert helped me through it. It took me at least a month to recover from my injuries. I had fractured bones and a bad concussion. I had to finish my schooling at home, thanks to my aunt and Jason, they came up with something that helped me, and wouldn't you know it I graduated from high school. Which is a miracle with everything that was going on in my life. A lot of university wanted me to attend their school, but I decided to take a year off and get a handle on my life. I know it is the wrong thing to do to miss school for a year, but I do not think I could have focused much. Robert graduated with honors he got accepted to go to Loyola University in Chicago Illinois. Robert and I became a thing, that was cute for like a week. It just did not feel right. I know it is wrong, but I feel like I am somewhat falling in love with Mammon. I keep pushing that feeling off telling myself differently, but who am I kidding every time he says something that I think is sweet, I get lost. You would think I felt different or that I hated him for making me what I am or because he is a demon, but I do not. Robert reaction when he found out I was possessed was weird. He did not say much, but he was not angry either. I let him know two weeks after, with my aunt and Jason help.

I want to say that he slowly got use to the idea, but I do not think he fully invested emotionally which in all fairness neither did I. We slowly became more like best friends than a couple. I informed Robert that he had a demon soldier that followed him around. He said, I knew there was something there, but I could not see it. Believe me, he made himself known, he said with some fear in his voice. What I found intriguing is that the demon never possessed him just followed him around, I thought they could only roam around earth in human form, but I was wrong. Robert and I both decided that when school starts again, since he will be in Illinois and me in North Carolina it would be best if we stay as friends. Let's be honest, nobody does long distance relationship, not even ones that was beginning to fall apart before it even got started.

My aunt and Jason Reynolds the Chief of police are planning their wedding which will be in July. I am overly excited about this; this is the one normal thing in our lives. I am so proud of my aunt despite everything going on she has gotten everything under control, she has matured, and I am proud to have Jason as my uncle. I know he has our back for everything, and I know he is hoping that nothing will ruin his wedding, with any of our secret weirdness. On a higher note, in mid-September Mammon performed an exorcism and removed a demon from my grandmother. Something new that I learned is that demons can perform exorcisms also. Believe me when I say it was not easy and not for the faint of heart either. In my mind I did not think my grandmother would have survived. This is where I am going to begin the next chapter of my chaotic life.

I have been in my room for months and I was ready to smell fresh air and feel the sun rays touch my skin. It was a Saturday I remember it was the first day of me feeling good enough to move around. I had a cast on my arm and bandages around my ribs, I had finish getting ready and was ready to start my day. I began to walk towards the stairs when I heard a woman cry. It stopped me in place, I felt a cold shiver run down my spine. I turned my head slowly and looked over at my grandparent's room. I watched the door start to open slowly, hearing the creeks of the door makes the darkness coming from the room even more intense. This all seemed way too Familiar, I thought to myself. The cry got louder as the door opened, I felt every hair on my arm stand straight up. Last time something like this happened both my grandparents and I got possessed, with the door only opened halfway; I could not see anything in the room. I squinted my eyes to try and see something, I was so focused and concentrated on seeing any outlines of something that I jumped back when I finally noticed a set of eyes just staring at me. I must have triggered something because Mammon immediately came forward and said, "what is that?" "What is going on?"

"Shh", I told him. "I am not sure I spotted those eyes a couple of seconds ago." My mind still has not caught up to process what I saw, I started to tremble a little, I knew what I had to do, but thinking it and doing it are two different things. I slowly began to move towards my grandparents' room. I was afraid something was going to jump out and run towards me at full speed. Without realizing it I was falling into a hypnosis from those eyes inside the room. "those eyes?" "They look so familiar" but astrain at the same time. I broke myself out of the trans and realized I was right at the bedroom door. The cry of the woman was so loud inside the room, it was more like a high-pitched cry that made me lose my focus, I held on to the door frame and on the wall, I thought I was about to pass out. Then the cry and the high pitch noise stopped, it took me a couple of minutes to get myself together. Once I was focused again, I got some bravery and started to walk in.

The minute I stepped my foot in the room, I heard whimpers, the whimpers sounded weird like if there were two voices in one. I could not quite describe the feeling I had it was as if one of the voices was so familiar. I took two more steps, and the voice went from whimpering to laughing. My heart skipped a beat, I quickly merged with my demon Mammon and transformed. With my transformation I was able to use enhance vision and quickly adjusted to the darkness. I quickly responded, "who is there?" "Come out and reveal yourself."

A voice from within the darkness came through and said, "You do not have that power to command me", the thing said. I quickly scanned the room to see where the voice was coming from, but still could not see anything. I walked further into the room and as soon as I reached the middle of the room, I felt a cold burst of air and the door behind me closed. I jumped and hollered a little, that literally almost made my body lose all functions. Mammon quickly stated, "calm down, do not get over worked." "Whatever is here does not sound easy to take down." "Give me a minute, I am going to heighten our sight"

As soon as he said that the room drastically has changed. It was as if I had night vision and special goggles to see outside of my realm. I could see things crawling on the wall, but it was as if they did not see us at all. I kept looking around and then I spotted those eyes, I know we made contact because I could feel those eyes piercing through my soul. "Come out and show yourself?" I said again, it did not respond, it just stared. I got angry so I said "I will not ask again". It started to laugh and that made every hair on my arms, back and leg stand straight up, It made my bone shake; I was petrified with fear. I was afraid, but I was compelled to walk forward. The creature stopped laughing when I got mid-way to it. Then it spoke, "I sense something about you that is different".

"Master?" It said sounding confused. I was going to respond as if he knew exactly who it was, and mammon quickly responded before I could, "Xonor is that you?" Once the creature heard his voice it slowly came out from underneath my grandparent's bed. Slowly and careful it started to reveal itself, my heart literally skipped a beat when I see what came out, it was my grandmother. I got this lump in my throat and I had to push my tears back, she looked like she has been starving, burses all down her arms and legs, cuts on her face and pale as if her body never seen sunlight. It took a lot for me to hold in my cry, but I did. Mammon quickly said to me "do not cry, be strong you do not want to show weakness".

I shock off the bad thoughts, took two deep breaths and stood my ground. It kept turning its head side to side almost scanning me to make sure it did not make a mistake. "Master!", It finally yelled out, it sounded excited to hear him. "Why haven't you fully possessed her yet, master?" "I am trying something different" Mammon told him, "once I am done, I will take her over." It does not surprise me anymore, the things that my demons say, but I do sometimes wonder. I did not really react to that I knew he was lying. He started laughing and said, "the human has turned you". I could not believe what I just heard, was he making fun of Mammon? His so-called master. He laughed again, "I could help you turn this human into your toy". That infuriated me, to hear the crap that was coming out of its mouth, but I kept it together and let it speak.

"We need to get him out of her", I told Mammon. "I know", he responded "it is not going to be easy", He sounded very frustrated. "What do you want to do?" I said with a little attitude. "Let me handle this", he told me with this very eerie tone. "Xonor, why would I the prince of hell need help from a mere runt like you?" "I am quite capable in obtaining my human, but you on the other hand have lost everything I taught you." "You look horrible, the body is starting to smell and decompose." "You need a new one my old friend." "Master, do not be mean I have been touring this woman for a year, she is a strong old bat." Xonor said sounding ashamed. I felt a ball of anger starting to rise I was ready to explode. "Now, now Xonor playing with your food is wrong even in our world." I heard him smirk. Really! Okay I was wrong my demon could still surprise me, I am going to kill him myself. "Now, my old friend let us go hunting for a more suitable food suite that you could use, being a woman is so not your style, as these retched humans say." Xonor laughed.

"I do not believe it is you master; the prince of hell would never ask such things of me nor think that my torture methods would be wrong." I heard Mammon's voice change and the sternness scared me. "Xonor do not make this harder than it should be, obey me or I will have no choice but to fight you." a flash of red is what I saw, I could tell Mammon was showing his domains. "Aww, so there is my master" Xonor said with way too much delight. "Now master let us fight," Xonor smiled exposing those long pointy and sharp teeth covered with black tar. The black tar just spouting out of its mouth dripping, it was disgusting and smelled like dead flesh. "Fine let us begin," Mammon said without hesitation. Mammon took over my body completely and my soul was hidden in his home on his bed, again. So, he decided to fight Xonor alone, that is really starting to annoy me," We are better together" I yelled. We might have lost one fight, but I think we could of both took care of this. Then it hit me like a lightning strike, they were battling in my grandparents' room, "Oh shit!" my aunt.

The whole time I paced back and forth, it felt like an eternity, but it was only an hour that passed by. I was starting to lose my cool and I was seconds from yelling out when Mammon comes in through a red door that was not there before. He looked tired, sweaty, and very bloody. I went from angry to worried and I quickly ran to him. I grabbed his hand walked him over to the bed and laid him down. "What happened?" I said, "it was hard, but I managed to tie him up and settle him down." "Of course, your aunt heard all the commotion upstairs and she helped." "Xonor is right he continued; I have become soft since I've meet you." Well dang, okay that hurt a little. I really wanted to knock him across the head, but I refrained because he looked terrible already. "Hey, do not take this out on me, you placed me here, I had faith we could had taken him together, but no, you had no faith in us" he did not reply to that all he could say was "I need to rest now. Go and help your aunt keep him under control, it is going to be a long day." I rolled my eyes and stormed out of the room going through that red door he appeared in, that was the first wrong thing I did. Going Through that door at first darkness, complete blackness and the feeling of loneliness was overwhelming. Then it is like opening your eyes through someone else life. It was weird, when I got all my barring together, I sat up and immediately got sick. I struggled to get up and I knew I was not going to make it to the bathroom. So, I found a trash can and let it all out. I was throwing up so hard that it looked like my abdominal area what being sucked out; I was throwing up so hard I literally farted. "I will never take that door again", I said out loud.

I got an old dirty shirt I found on the floor and wiped my mouth clean I started to look around and I noticed I was in my room on my bed, finally I felt pain. I looked down and noticed I had a bandage on my side; I quickly ran my finger threw my bandage and felt the stitches. I started to pan around the room, and I got startled when I see my aunt just sitting on a small couch next to my bed. "Aunty, are you okay?" She had this mean face, like she was ready to flip crap. "I cannot believe this shit is happening again!" "Aunties wait, I could explain." "STOP!!" She yelled at me; "I do not think I could do this again." "Aunty its grandma I know she is in there still alive fighting, I heard that thing say so. We have to try and help her." "No Yamaries that is not grandma anymore that thing is well...," she paused to think of what exactly to call it. I did not blame her I do not know what to call it. "Well, she continued; I have no idea what it is, but I can tell you it is not grandma." "She is in there give me and Mammon a chance, we could get her back." "Aunty he is very convinced that he can."

"Yamaries, I have that thing tied up on my mom and dad's bed, if I did not think both of you could do it, I would not have helped, he convinced me he could." "I trust him he better not let me down." My aunt changed her tone from really upset to calm and collective, her mood swings are giving me a headache. "When are you planning on starting? I have no idea how long these protection spells are going to work, or the ropes holding for that matter." "Aunty, Mammon is hurt he said he needs a little bit of time, but we will start the extraction today. Right now, we are taking shifts to sit with it and guard it to make sure nothing goes wrong until we could start."

"Okay fine let us get this started" she said, "I will take first watch aunty and a couple hours you will take over, hopefully he will be ready before you will take over." "Okay I will be downstairs cleaning the kitchen call me if you need me." I watched her get up and walked out my room I could see she was frustrated, angry and annoyed. I am quite sure she just wanted a year without mayhem, I felt bad and a little selfish, I just wanted my grandmother back I needed her back. I gathered my thoughts and my nerves to walk over to my grandparent's room. I got up from the bed slowly and began walking over to my grandparent's room, it felt like I was walking through the halls of death row, thinking of all my past doings, and getting ready to get the lethal injection. Once I got to the bedroom door I froze, I knew what was inside, I knew once I seen her it was going to hurt. I slowly opened the door and started to walk in I could hear the heavy breathing. The slowly long inhales and the harsh exhales, I walked all the way inside the room and seen that she was tied to the bed, that killed me. I wanted to cry but I did not, I did not want to show any weakness.

Every time I looked over at her I did not see it; I see my grandmother's beautiful smile and her eyes that said everything. I walked over to the bed and pulled a chair close. I did as my impulse told me to do and I grabbed her hand and just watched her asleep. I wonder how hard he hit her, it was not the same anymore she had cuts on her face, and she was cold and clammy. I went into a deep thought and started to remember when grandma use to caresses my face and I could feel her soft hands moving across my face and hearing her tell me how much I look like my mother. This high-pitched laugh startled me back into reality. I slowly opened my eyes and looked up; it was staring at me with those yellow and black eyes this smile almost loving my torture. I looked into its dark hallow eyes and seen nothing but my pain. "Oh, poor little Yamaries miss your grandma little girl?" It laughed at me and it kept pushing my buttons. "Your pathetic, you will never have her back." "You made him weak, he will never be able to return to hell." It tried to jump at me but the rope and the magic spell my aunt did yanked it back.

"You think these ropes, or this weak magic spell is going to hold me, well not for long." I did not say a word just stared I do not want to give it a chance to feel like it is getting under my skin. "Well, Well looks like my master has been teaching you well, no combat, no responses or maybe I have not said the right thing yet." He kept taunting me for hours. Each time making my blood boil, I felt like I was ready to pop. What he said next through me over the edge, "I have your grandmother in here wishing she were dead. She keeps begging me to kill her, it is so much fun when they beg." I lost it and jumped out of my seat and went to charge at it when this force pushed me down. I got confused because I knew that creature was tied up and it had barrier around it, so it could not have been him. "What the hell?" Was the only thing I conjured up to say. "NO! Yamaries you should not touch him or give into his taunts; this is his torture methods." "This is what brings him pleasure." "Mammon? Aren't you supposed to be getting some rest?" I said with confusion. "I am doing better, and I was listening to everything." "You heard everything and did nothing?" "Why would you let me go through all this torment?"

"Yamaries, you did very well, you have endured a lot with his taunt, and you took it for hours, most people would have crack, but you did not." "If we are ever in a battle and I get rendered unconscious, how will I know if you could endure so much pain?" "This day you have shown me that you could take anything that comes your way." "I also want to let you know that a greater Demon is far more powerful." It was wording like those that made me wonder if we could be more than human and demon. "Mammon", it called out to him, "its master to you and do not forget that." He said with authority "I will call you master when you deserve to be called that, right now you are neither my master nor my ally." "We need to call your aunt up here it is time, let us begin this exorcism." "Xonor you are going home where you shall pay for your insolence." Mammon called for my aunt through my thoughts, she came quickly you could tell she was ready, so it has begun.

<u>*Chapter Two*</u>

Mammon hovered over Xonor and began chanting, "eminus extraous averba" and this heaviness came over the room almost like if something was applying pressure on my body. "Envois numerous Encanto", he kept repeating these words sometimes I forget that he is me, so when I hear his chant, I do not hear that it is my voice. I looked at Xonor and he was in pain I could tell by the thrashing and the yelling. "NO! Master do not do this, I could help you please", all mammon did was answer with another chant. "Ominous emous nasfura". Xonor let out the biggest roar, it sounded so painful. I could not help but feel a little bad; I never knew that it would be that painful for a demon to be exercised by another demon with their words. "You will never be able to return home master; you will forever stay here with these humans." "Fortusa, Xantaro, encantor", Mammon yelled. These chants and thrashing went on for literally three days straight. On the third day my aunt and I were ready to give up and just let Xonor have my grandmother's body.

Before He began on the fourth day Mammon looked at me and my aunt and said, "please do not give up just yet, I could do this.' My aunt's eyes said it all; I know she wants to give up, so I said what I think my aunt wanted to say. "No, I think we should stop and give up." "What condition will my grandmother's body be in?" "Will she survive this without begin traumatized?" "Remember she has been taken over for a year." I explained to him. "I know you feel helpless ladies I really do but I could do this." "If your grandmother is in there, she will fight to for the chance to see you one more time." He sounded so confident and sweet, "We will give it one more try and then if this does not work, we are done, it is over." My aunt who was quite for the most part quickly answered with "yes, I agree if it does not work, we need to stop, kill her and it and bury my mother's body." "She needs peace and I need closure, let us get this day started." "Let us begin" Mammon said in agreeance with my aunt, we walked into the room, and quickly Xonor started laughing, "Mammon" he said, "you have gotten weak and soft." "You will never enter hell again; your father will be extremely disappointed, but do not worry Mammon I think your sister might do a better job ruling hell." Wait, I was very confused he has a sister? I wanted to ask him so many questions, but he was fully concentrated on the exorcism, he was determined not to lose. "Somor, Efubita, Nosvios, Commor, esfurta, Encarto". Something strange started to happen. The room temperature dropped drastically. "Amous, Menus, derudas". These words were a little different than the last, I am not sure why, but I got this weird feeling we were not at my home. The room looked like my grandparents' room but different, I could not really explain it. "Dasmenos, Lemuerde, orfurnia", My grandmother's body started to rise. I started to get this burning sensation, through my veins. It was painful, "Venous, Ensandeo, Kukuro". This flame came from my hands it was blue and tingly. I could feel my whole body starting to hurt as if I were changing. The burning sensation has gotten worse, and I felt as if I was going to pass out from the pain. I kept fighting that sensation, "Demenous, Xtratos, Enous". The room shook and this loud hurdling scream came from Xonor, I could tell that this was it. "Xonor!" Mammon said with a dominate voice, "say hi to dad", He said with a smirk on him. As he said that last incantation "Remoudes, Extranos", you could see Xonor true form come out of my grandmother, the bed fell into a big whole of flames. I watched as Xonor screamed and fell into the flaming pit of hell. Slowly the whole began to close, and the room was going back to normal. The room began to shake a little as if it was trying to place the pieces back in the right spot. The bed I taught was swallowed by the flames was back in the room and my grandmother's body slowly descended on it, I wanted to run and huge her and wake her up. It was as if Mammon knew what I wanted to do and said, "ladies do not rush her, give her some time to recover, remember she had a foreign entity that took over." "She must slowly come back and get everything working like it used to, it is going to be a long and tiring process, be patient with her."

He was right I was just very impatient; I remember in the movies how demons when exercised the human starts healing fast, but this was not a movie, and my grandmother did not heal quickly. She looked as if she has been through hell and back, it is crazy I never thought for a minute how difficult it would be to nurse her back to health. My aunt never left my grandmother's side while she was recovering. When my aunt needed a break, she'll call me and have me stay with her, I offered for us to take shifts and while she was recovering but my aunt wanted to do it her way and I didn't argue. She is always doing what I want and then she cleans up my mess, so I did not argue. When Jason found out about my grandmother, at first, he was a little upset that she was there the whole time and we never told him. Then he started to get better and was happy we were okay and nothing bad happened. He did help us take care of her, he sat with my aunt and watched over my aunt. I know my aunt is waiting patiently for my grandmother to make any kind of movement.

As we were dressing her up and replacing her bandages, a month after her long exorcism. I felt my grandmother move her hand. I stopped and quickly called out to my aunt. "Look, I think she is moving." My aunt's eyes quickly looked at my grandmother's hand and they once again moved. My aunt's eyes quickly filled with tears and so were mines. My grandmother made a noise, and my heart skipped a beat; she was trying to shift her body, but we quickly held her to make sure she didn't make a move that could reopen some of her wounds. "Grandma" I said softly with a lot of hope in my voice, she kept moaning and trying to shift but she did not answer me. "Mom", my aunt said, "please stop moving you are going to hurt yourself." "Grandma, can you hear us?" "Yamaries?" My grandmother said, "yes grandma it is me and aunty is here to." "Ana?" 'Yes, mom it is me", my aunt could not hold it and started to cry. She was crying so hard that I had a hard time keeping myself from crying that hard to. My grandmother tried to talk a little more, but nothing came out. My aunt quickly responded to that and said "mom, do not talk just rest and recover I am going to be here, and I will never leave you, I promise." I was filled with so much joy and happiness; it felt like my heart was going to explode with excitement. I looked over at my aunt and I could tell she was overjoyed; she had not smiled that big since, well dang last year. Even when she got engaged, she did not smile this big. Some of the emptiness in our hearts, were beginning to fill, I wish my grandfather were here to see how we worked so hard to bring grandma back and we never gave up hope. My aunt looked at me and mouthed out "thank you" still smiling that beautiful smile holding my grandmother, I smiled back at her and mouthed back "I love you". I smiled and slowly walked out of the room, it felt good to know I gave my aunt something to be proud of. I closed the door to the room to give my aunt and grandmother some alone time.

I walked over to my room with a big smile, I opened my door and walked over to my bed, I am not sure why, but my room looked brighter today than it has ever had. I through myself on my bed and laid there thinking about everything great that is going to happen now that my grandmother is back. With all this happens and excitement with my grandmother being back I have forgotten that without my demon Mammon none of this would have been possible, I just closed my eyes and thought about his room and that beautiful fireplace. I suddenly felt my room change and I knew I was not in mine any longer, I could feel the nice warmth of the fireplace on my skin, and I could smell the wood burning. I do love that smell and I could feel the nice silk sheets of his bed, he is an awfully expensive demon. With my eyes still closed I heard his voice in my ear saying, "is everything okay?" His voice was so soft today and sweet or it could have been me just in tuned with my feelings. With my eyes still closed I answered "yes, I just wanted to see you." I turned my face and my body to face his, and I slowly opened my eyes. I know that this is not his true form, but his eyes are still beautiful. That nice ocean blue with a small hint of emptiness and a splash of intrigued. He smiled and said, "you should not be here, you should be with your grandmother and aunt." "No, I Am right where I want to be right now." For a split second I think I seen something like feelings. I did not feel awkward or uncomfortable lying right next to him on his bed. This is strange to say, but it felt like this is where I belong. "My grandmother finally moved today, she managed to say my name and my aunts name." "I am glad she is starting to get strength she is a tough human, just like your aunt and you." That is exactly what I am talking about the words he uses, and he does not even know how much I am falling.

"You know it would not be possible without your help, Thank you so much." Without thinking I leaned in closed my eyes and kissed him. That is what every normal person would do, the reaction I got was not one I was expecting. He leaned back and said: what was that?" "Oh, I am so sorry, I did not mean……. I mean it is, well it," I could not finish my sentence I was so embarrassed and tripping over my words until finally I said, "it is called a kiss." I cannot believe I did that, why? Now he is going to get all weird and awkward. To top off everything, I know my face is red, I look like a tomato. He looked confused, which scared me, "so humans do that a lot?" Great here we go, "well yes, but they do not always mean the same thing." It was a little frustrating having to explain to him the emotions of humans, it kills that special meaning, but I brushed it off. So, I started to explain, "sometimes when someone kiss another person either it be female or male it could mean four things."

"The first meaning is Hello which is commonly used along with goodbye which is number two." "When we received something from a loved one, like a gift it could mean thank you which is number three." "Number four is the most complicated of them all, because sometimes when you give someone a kiss this way you run the chance of them not feeling that way." I tried explaining. "which mean is that?" He asked, "I love you."

"Sometimes this word is thrown out there for fun because sometimes humans could be cruel to one another but when it is really meant you could feel it. It is something that runs through you like fire and excitement, and you could just see it radiate through." He did not answer right away, I think he might have been taking it all in. "Humans are filled with so many emotions, your overly complex creatures." HUH? I thought to myself, did he just called me a creature, I am not sure how to take that. I know he does not understand, and I know he is not human but that made me feel uncertain and confused." It is funny how one gesture could have so many meanings, how is it that one could really interpret what it means?" Wow he is interested in this topic, I never meant for it to be explained in this much detailed, but I am glad at least he is not thinking about the one I just gave him. "Well normally us humans have emotions we could tell by their demeanor and the way they deliver the kiss." "Before the kiss is delivered there will be body movement of some sort and facial expressions that would give the other person a hint." "Sometimes people get it wrong and that is okay, not everyone is in tune with those emotions."

Sometimes it hard for me to know what he is thinking but he looks very confused, I think I made it worse. "Humans are very confusing creatures indeed," and just when I thought this conversation was over and he has forgotten that I have given him a kiss he went and asked me the one question I was dreading the most. "Yamaries, I know you know that I am not human, and I cannot really interpret what your kiss means, are you going to let me know what yours meant?" "Umm…. well…..." I felt myself shrink and my heart drop to my stomach, I was stuck, I was scared and nervous. Okay, I could do this. I am a big girl, "well it meant two things." "Two huh?" he seemed very intrigued. "Well, I guess I am lucky" he said which in return made me laugh. He is getting use to this human stuff after all, "one it meant thank you. I really do appreciate everything you have done not just in save my grandmother but in opening my eyes to something different, scary but different than the normal." I was hoping with that he would go into more of me explaining what that meant but he did not. I think he really did understand that "and the second meaning to the kiss?" He asked staring at my eyes which made me so nerves. I would say he was staring at my soul, if it wasn't already exposed. How can I tell him that, it's wrong I shouldn't care about him like that, from the minute he showed his true form to me, weird things started happening scary things to be exact and I lost both my grandparents, even after all of that I feel this way and I can't keep it from him any longer? I closed my eyes and said, "I love you", it took him a little to answer me back, I opened my eyes, and he was staring at me, looking into my eyes as if he was investigating if I was telling a lie. He finally spoke and said "I am glad to hear that" like he understood what I meant. I had to admit at first it took me by surprise when he answered that, but I am wondering now if he is answering as if a human would.

"Do you know what I mean by that?" I asked and then quickly having regrets, "Somewhat" he said, "I think from other humans I took over." "There was once this woman I took over and possessed and there was this man and he fought for her and cried till the very end." "She had this certain feeling when she seen him like butterflies and tickling feeling it was weird and nice all at the same time." "Every time you see me, I feel that in your stomach area. He sounded like a little kid explaining himself. I smiled at him and said, "you are correct that is exactly what love is." "Well, Yamaries I think I am in love with you too." I turned red and got all tingly inside, "thank you' he said. "Why?' I answered. "For showing me that I can love. After that conversation I spent the rest of the day relaxing with him. The next day I realized that I only seen his true form once in the beginning when he was tormenting me. I really cannot remember what he looks like, If I am going to love him in full, I need to love all of him, the good and the bad, this might be something easily said than done.

I finally got the to spend some time with my grandma talking to her and her mostly listening. I do have to admit she normally did that anyways. She was all smiles, and I took in every minute of it. My grandmother has been moving around healing so much, unfortunately, two weeks after her awakening, Jason came into the house and told my aunt that he couldn't cover anymore, and we had to bring grandma back to the institute and let them reevaluate her. That broke my heart we had to sit down with her and let her know what was going to happen next. I listened as my aunt and Jason explained, she is such a strong woman, she smiled at us and said, "I understand." It was a rough three weeks for all of us, she wanted to be home, and We wanted her back. There was a glimmer of light while she was there, we were able to see her and speak to her until visiting hours was over. It was an exciting day when the doctor told my aunt that we could bring her home. I wanted to cry, the doctor told my aunt that she has come a long way and it is as if she has completely changed. I looked at my aunt and she did the same. We both new that my grandmother has changed.

The day we brought my grandmother home. We picked her up from the clinic and placed her in the car, the whole drive home my grandmother was quiet. She stared at everything almost as if she were seeing everything for the first time. She looked as if she wanted to cry, it must hurt knowing she has lost a whole year of her life. Once we pulled up to the house her eyes widen up and she finally spoke. "Our house has changed." My aunt and I were confused by her statement, "Huh? Grandma what do you mean?" "I could tell that things are not going to be the same." Just like that she opened the car door and got out. I looked at my aunt and said, "is it me or was that weird?" "No, no that was weird' she said. We quickly got out of the car and got inside the house I had a few questions for my grandmother. "Grandma?" I called out. "Grandma, where are you?" "I am over here in the kitchen" she answered sounding as if she was in full concertation. "Grandma, is everything okay?" My aunt and I walked into the kitchen and we both sat down. "Mom, what is it?" My aunt looked really concern that my grandmother had something going on like last time. "Girls, you have no idea the torment I went thru. How much I fought". "I kept telling myself that I will see you both again." "The room he kept me in was horrible, the cries of other souls the smell of death was unbearable." "There were times where I just wanted to give up, but I pulled myself together and said my girls need me." There were even times I thought I heard both of you yelling my name calling out for me. Those days I fought hard and at one point I thought he got a little tired but the next day it would wear me down." "I am so sorry girls that I am acting weird or lost, I just thought I will never see this place again or either of you for that matter." "When you two helped me escape I tell you what I was minutes of letting go, but it is funny I heard both of your voices, but a strange young man came and helped me out." "It must have been something I thought up."

I could not believe the torment my poor grandmother went through all alone. I knew she was a fighter and was waiting for us. I am glad we showed up just in time. I looked over at my aunt and she was crying, but not one of those cute cry's it was the big ugly ones with just a little bit of boogers coming down her nose. "I am so sorry mom; we should have come for you sooner or fought for you harder." "I never wanted you to feel any pain or loneliness. I promise mom I will always be by your side." "Good", my grandmother said, "I do not want either of you leaving my side." "Now, which one of you is going to tell me where your grandfather is?" My eyes opened wide; I look like a deer caught in headlights. I looked over at my aunt quickly to see if she would respond but she looked just as dumb founded as me. "Grandma", I started might as well since most of this stuff started because of me. "Umm, well grandpa died grandma while you were possessed by that demon." "I am so sorry grandma," my grandmother placed her hand down and started to cry. "I had a feeling", she answered 'I did not ask until now because I was afraid to hear it out loud". "It hurts to know I could not help him; I wonder if he was just as scared as I was." "No", she quickly said "not my Juan he was always the brave one". 'Your grandfather was" and she smiled within those tears, I could not help but cry to, I could feel and hear how much my grandmother loved my grandfather. "Did I ever tell you girls that your grandpa and I we were partner in crime?" "I know your grandpa since we were kids, we did everything together good and bad when we were kids, we laughed and grew old together." He was, no he is and will always be my soul mate." "I do not want to accept that I have lost him forever."

Suddenly without any warning mammon spoke to me. "He is not lost forever; he is held in a special place." "I told you a while back that your grandfather was touched by angels." "He had special gifts I am sure your grandfather gave him a good run in that battle but Zozo would have never killed his soul." "The body yes but his soul that is too powerful." "What do you mean?" I asked him, "People like your grandfather are rare. He is pure, meaning his soul was meant to stay with god never to enter a human body but somehow it did." "Those souls we cannot destroy. We look for them as long as I could remember, for souls like are hard to come by." "If I know Zozo he has your grandfather soul somewhere hidden in a special place. If we try, I think we can find him." I was so confused in why he wanted to help. "Why do you care so much about my grandfather soul?" "Because" he said, "there is something different about your grandmother's love for your grandfather that is so pure and very intriguing". "In all my years of possession I learned what different loves and hate is but this one is so different, its real". I have never heard him sound so honest and extremely interested, but the fact that he wants to help still has me confused. Before I realized it, I had my grandmother and my aunt staring at me. My aunt was looking at me like she wanted to kick my ass, my grandmother looked confused. I stared at them and said "yeah, why are all staring at me like that?" My grandmother was the first to respond, "we have been calling your name for twenty minutes with no response from you, you look like you were in a trance." "Is everything okay, honey?" How was I going to break it to my grandmother that I been possessed and taken over by a demon that has not tortured me in any way that she was. I do not know how she will take it, just knowing I am possessed, and I am okay with it. So, I did the next best thing, "grandma I'm fine a lot has happened, and a lot of information was thrown in the air I must process, so that is why I was in my own little world." My aunt rolled her eyes at me, and my grandmother did not buy that at all.

"Yamaries do not lie to me", she was mad. How can she tell, "what?" I managed to say. "Do not lie I have been through a lot with that demon torture and lying to me, I would have never excepted it from you.' I lowered my head and said, "your right grandma I am so sorry", I felt so bad and guilty, I do not know why I thought my grandmother would not be able to handle it. She has been through so much. "Okay, I have to tell you something but do not freak out". "You have been possessed", she said. My mouth flew open, how did she know. "Yamaries, I felt him since I came back, you will be surprised what you can learn and what you could feel after being possessed." "He is different than the others," I tried explaining. "yes, grandma he is." "He did not force me or torture me" He did trick me so to say, I said to myself. "He has not really taken over; he is more like…" "sharing, right? My grandmother asked. She scares me every time she does that, "yeah grandma something like that." "Okay then why haven't you tried to remove him?" "Grandma he is not bad at all, he helped get you out of there." "Yamaries I am not sure if I will be able to trust him like you do." She Turned to my aunt "Ana honey do you trust him?" "Well mom yes as of right now he has not failed me or Yamaries." "In the last year he has… She trailed off, "WOW!" She stopped in the middle of her sentence. "I never really thought about it until now, but he has really help us through a lot she looked at me and smiled." "Yes, he has" I said with a smile. "Mom I completely understand if you do not trust him right now, that is okay but please do not be closed off give him a chance." My grandmother just looked at us and knotted her head and agreed. "Now, you two I am going to bed, I need a nap and time to take all this in, I think you two should to." "I am home now, and things are going to be different." "Okay grandma gets some rest," I wanted to tell her what mammon told me, but she looks like she had a long day, and I really don't think she'll believe or trust what he has to say just yet.

We watched my grandmother go upstairs and into her room, I quickly turn to my aunt and said, "I must tell you something." "Oh no, Yamaries I know that look, you are going to suggest something dangerous." "Huh? Aunty that hurts, I would…." I stopped in mid-sentence "okay whatever. Anyway, Mammon said that grandpa is not dead." "Really Yamaries! For goodness's sake we seen his body." "Yes, his body but not his soul." "Yamaries what are you talking about?" "Grandpa was pure, he was touched by an angel which means his soul is pure, mammon says that Zozo could have his soul somewhere." "Yamaries, look at me I know what you're going to suggest, and the answer is NO." "I just got mom back, I'm working on my wedding venues, my fiancé is busy with work and I have work to do." "Young lady one, you do not have proof of these, and two mammon does not either, all of this are theories." "I want mom to have some normalcy right now." "But aunty…." "NO! Yamaries no." "She just went through a lot I do not want her going through a wild goose chase." "I do not want to bring up her hopes of finding dad and get nothing in return. The pain she will go through is something I do not want her to ever bear, and she does not deserve that." "I also advice for you to please not mention any of that to her." I was angry at what she was saying, I did understand that grandma has been through a lot and I do not want to give her false hope, but she was completely blowing this off. I just want both to be okay and grandpa goes to the place he needs to be. So, all I could do was say "Okay aunty I will not", I knew she was not going to change her mind. "Thank you, and Yamaries?" "Yes aunty", "do not merge with Mammon in front of grandma right now." I lost my cool, "Well Damn, okay anything else. Should I stay in my room I do not want to get in her way". She really pissed me off, I walked past her and went up the stairs to my room. I left her downstairs trying to tell me something, but I really did not care what she wanted to tell me, I walked into my room and shut the door. I through myself on my bed, AHHH! I screamed into my pillow kicking my feet against the bed. I need to escape, I need my paradise, I closed my eyes and thought about him and his place. This is my happy place.

Chapter Three

The Next morning, I felt like it was going to be awkward around my grandmother, I do not want her not to trust me because mammon has partial possession of me. I wanted her to know and understand that mammon and I are partners, and we work together. I walked downstairs and I heard her scuffling around in the kitchen. I am going to talk to her and help her understand. I walked in the kitchen and seen that my grandma has been busy cooking up a storm, "morning grandma", I said with a smile. "Good morning my love, how did you sleep last night?" She had this beautiful smile and this ease about her, I knew she was happy to be home after everything. "Okay I guess, Grandma can we talk?" She stopped what she was doing and had a look of concern. "You could always talk to me, what is on your mind?" "I want you to believe that mammon is on our side." "Yamaries, I believe and trust you, but please do not force me to trust a demon." "I will not be made or accept something that I was forced to do." "Grandma I am not…." she cut me off quickly and she was angry. "STOP! I do not want to talk about it anymore." My grandmother got so upset she walked out of the kitchen and straight upstairs; she has never yelled at me like that before. I could not even give her my peace; I was never going to force her I just wanted to let her know that she could trust in my judgement. I knew she went in her room because I heard her door slam. I felt bad, I did not mean to upset her. My grandmother must have woken up my aunt when she slammed the door because my aunt came downstairs ready to kill me. "What is wrong with you?" I looked so confused "Huh?" "Why are you upsetting her?" "Aunty, I did not do it on purpose, I was just trying to get her to trust…." Once again, she cut me off, my aunt seems to like doing that a lot lately and I hate that. "NO! Yamaries, she does not have to do anything." "She is confused, she lost her husband, and her only granddaughter is possessed and let me remind you that the demon that possessed her was not as nice as your mammon, so no she doesn't have to do anything." "She needs things to go to normal, can you do that?" I hate when she talks to me like that, "yeah, I can do that." "Good, now I am going back to bed because I have a lot to do later." "Okay, I will go to my room to." My aunt turned around and walked up the stairs, I swear I thought I seen steam coming out of her head.

At that point I did not want to stay at the house, so I decided to go for a walk. I really did not pay much attention where I was walking, I just needed to walk. I figured I had my phone I could GPS it later. I went through every conversation that day and quickly came to the conversation with mammon, "his physical form is dead, but his soul is not, he is being held in a special place". It played repeatedly in my mind, I knew I had to do something, I know now it had to be without my grandmother and aunt. As my mind is going in a circle trying to figure things out, I did not realize I was in the woods and I do mean I was deep in the woods.

Still in full concentration I heard a noise like a twig snapping. I jumped and was in full panic mode. I did not transform because it could easily be a person. I looked around and scanned my area. The first thing that came to mind was man dang I am in the middle of the woods and I do not know how to get out. "Crap", I said out loud. I kept looking around making sure nothing would catch me off guard. As I was standing still trying to listen out for any noise from the corner of my eye, I seen something run across and go behind me. I quickly turn around in the place of where the sound came from and seen absolutely nothing. From my left side I heard another tree branch snap, I quickly partially transformed I knew something was out there that was not a person. I heightened my senses, I needed to see what was out there no more hiding. I scanned the area again, "come out, come out, wherever you are". I said to myself, I got you, it was trying to hide behind a tree, really is that what the underworld has come to. It was a skinny creature; I knew it was not something I seen before. I felt my whole body tense up when I saw the creature, but I knew not to show fear. I stood my ground and quickly said, "Hello?" "Who are you?" The creature fidgeted a little and then it pokes it head out from behind the tree. His face was a little gruesome, its face was pale with a slimy sustains secreting from its pours. It had all its teeth exposed, as I look closely, I noticed that the creature does not have any lips. That took my back I suddenly was too afraid to say anything else to the lipless creature. I knew I had to suck it up and be brave, mammon cannot do everything for me. "Hey, I am speaking to you". "Who are you?" "What do you want?" It did not say anything it just turned its head and looked confused. It suddenly darted from one tree to the other, I finally seen its full body, and it was insane. Its feet were as if placed backwards almost like a wolf. Its torso sucked in curling underneath its ribs and the rib cage was sticking out. Its hand was long, skinny with purple black nails. His arms look so long it looked like it could rap its arm around a tree. I felt my heart skip a beat; "do not make me keep repeating myself". "This will be the last time and I will defend myself". "Who are you?" The thing looked at me with those black hallow eyes and said, "I am no one and everyone, and who might you be?" His voice was soothing and creepy at the same time, almost like a creepy lullaby. "Yamaries", I said, I really did not want to answer him, but I felt I had to. "Good Yamaries" it said, "now I need an answer from you". "Okay", I said "anything you need". Okay what is going on? Why am I answering everything he says? Wait, how did he get control of this situation that quickly? "Where is my master and friend from hell?" Huh, what is it talking about? "Who do you speak of?" I tried to stop myself from speaking but it is like I am in a weird trans, it was horrible. "I Speak of the prince from hell, but you might know him as Mammon".

It was like clockwork as soon as Mammon heard his name he appeared and the trans I was in was gone. "Who has summoned me?" I was no longer in control and neither was that thing. "Master!" It said, that scared me the last time I heard that the thing possessed my grandmother. "Loard?" "How can this be?" "Loard?" I asked him, "what is that?" He did not answer me and kept on his conversation with that thing. "What are you doing on the surface?" "Master, things have gotten bad down there". Well, that was the understatement of the world, its hell it supposed to be bad. "What do you mean?" "How has it gotten bad?" "Master, he is back, Zozo." I felt this intense heat boiling in my skin. "It cannot be he is running around in a human". "No, master the human body is in hell with him, and master he is back to his old tricks again". "Where is my father? He must know this is going on". "Master your father has disappeared.

He has been gone for a couple of weeks now and nobody knows where he is at". "Your sister has been controlling hell, with little to no respect from the others". His sister? He has a sister to. "Loard, you and the others do not underestimate my sister she is sinister and can be very scary." "That is exactly what I told them, master's little misses should not be played with, I seen her torture methods." "Why do you need me?" "Master leave this human and come home. You must rule hell, or everything will turn into chaos." "Yvi is your ruler", "NO! she is not, and you know the traditions". "She cannot rule, master everyone has heard the rumor that you have become close with the human". "HOW DARE YOU!!!" His roar shock me to the core, he is pissed. "I am sorry master, I was not trying to insult you, it will never happen again." This meeting was starting to be intense, and I felt like I was right in the middle of it. "Master, please forgive me, we need you to rule for the sake of hell." "Loard, go you will be summoned when I have my response." "Yes, master as you wish", Loard looked at him for a little bit before he left. His look was very piercing, almost as if he wanted to dig deep and reach me.

As we are following him through the woods, we realized that we ended up in the same spot where we had the battle. "I thought we closed that portal?" "I could feel it, but I cannot see it", "Me neither" mammon said, "I wonder" mammon was in deep thought. "Wonder what?" "What are you talking about?" "Yamaries, you need to think outside of the box." "Look around, last time the portal was visible where it was easily found." "Why would they make the same mistake twice?" "Your right, so let see if I were them and did not want anyone to know where I hide something important, where would I place it?" I kept walking around and noticed a small hill where you could crawl in and out of without anyone noticing. "Mammon" I said quickly, "there that is where the portal is at." "Underground where no one would ever crawl in". "Now what are we going to do?" "I am not sure he said but I do know that there is a lot of funny stuff going on right now." "Let us go home, strategies that is what we need to do right now." "I agree", I told him. We began walking out of the woods. "Mammon" I said "yes Yamaries?" "We must go to hell, one we need to rescue my grandfather's soul and two you need to go back home and rule, you do know, that right?" Mammon did not answer which was not like him at all, we walked all the way home in silence. That killed me I am not use to him speaking his mind or at least conversating about different topic. All these questions started to flood my mind, why is he so quiet? What can he be thinking about, so hard? It is a lot to take in, he must go home and rule, which he probably does not want to do. Can it be that he does not want to save my grandfather? It killed me not knowing, I walked through the front door and my aunt was sitting on the couch with my grandmother. They both turned to look at me and my grandmother was the first to respond. "Yamaries, there you are." "You scared me; I am not sure where you went." At first, I was a little confused because in my mind I was only gone for a couple of minutes, but I have been gone for five hours. Wow, I have never done that before without getting tired. "I am so sorry grandma I did not mean to scare you, I needed to clear my head." My aunt just stood there staring at me with this evil look, like I killed someone. "Granny I am sorry; I will try my best to let you know where I am at." "Please Yamaries, you and your aunt are all I have left, I do not, I cannot lose either of you." "I am so sorry grandma", I did feel horrible for making her worry, but I did not intentionally plan on scarring her.

Once I apologize for the fifth time and no words from my aunt, I walked up stairs and straight to my room. Normally I would talk to my aunt regarding things I just learned but lately she has been acting weird and not really wanting to talk or listen when it is about the supernatural or our abilities. I do find it funny how we humans wish we had some special ability like seeing ghosts or being able to open and close portals but what is funny is once they do get a little hint of it their whole world comes crumbling down. As I laid on my bed all these thoughts were flowing in my mind. Sometimes I wish I could just stop and sort of my thoughts and try to analyze one by one unfortunately I do not get that luxury. I was in deep through when I heard my door open, I must admit it scared the crap out of me. "Yamaries? Can I come in?" My aunt sounded worried. I hope she did not come here to yell or fuss because right now I am not in the mood, "yes aunty you could come in". She walked in and sat on my bed right next to me. "Yamaries, I do not want to make you upset, but you have been acting different. I am not sure what is going on, but you normally talk to me about everything". Really!? Did she just say I am acting different? No, she did not. I had to get myself together because I knew I was going to snap. So, I took two deep breaths and said, "No, there is nothing wrong with me, I just cannot get anyone to be happy with me these days." Well, I did try and not give an attitude, but it came out anyway. "Yamaries it is that attitude of yours, you are changing and not in a good way".

I could not hold back; I was upset that she was blaming only me. "Aunty you think I have changed but it is you, I have changed literally, and I am embracing what I am, I am never going to change". "You are acting as if it is not true everything that happen in the last year was fake". "News flash just because you ignore it that does not mean it will go away". "Yamaries what are you talking about?" "Nothing is happening you want to make something happen". "Aunty, mammon told us that grandpa's spirit could be in a special place that Zozo keeps in hell". "We could rescue his soul and you're acting like I am making it all up". "Yamaries, you do not know that to be true, so in a sense you are." "Really? Have I ever said anything that ever lead you wrong?" "When it comes to you and granny and grandpa, I will go to the deepest part of hell to save you all." "Listen to what you are saying? You cannot go down there it is not safe". "The last time you two went up against him you lost and that was with mammon's help". "This time you are going to take the fight in his world". "That is a whole other ball game, besides, we just got my mom, your grand mom back, I do not want to leave her again". "I cannot lose her I will not". "Aunty, you're holding on tight if you keep suffocating her, she is going to snap." "Come with me to hell lets save grandpa, let us do it for grandma". "Do not! Do that, do not use my mom as an excuse". "She will be happy knowing that he is soul is in heaven, you know that is where he belongs." "what does Mammon think about your endeavors?" "I am not sure when I was in the woods, we encounter another demon, he was looking for him telling him what is going on in hell". "Yamaries! There is another portal open?" "I thought I closed it". "You did the first one, but the creatures must have created another one, In a highly creative spot". "You mean to tell me they got smarter?" "Yep, they did, and they did it on the side of a hill where you have to crawl in." "That is crazy, I guess I must go close that portal". "No! Aunty you cannot, that is the way we could descent to hell". "Yamaries we are not going to hell". "We have a wedding to finish planning and now grandma needs a dress, we have a lot to do and plan". I knew I was not going to get anywhere with her right now, so I did what I thought was right at the time lie. "Your right aunty we have a lot of other stuff we must prepare for." My aunt's eyes lit up, she smiled from ear to ear. I felt so bad lying to her, but it is for her own good. "Thank you, my love now get some rest and we will discuss all this wedding stuff tomorrow." "Grandma is going to be so excited." "yes, she is, I cannot wait." I put on a fake smile and she got up and walked out feeling proud of herself.

I laid back down and just closed my eyes. I really was trying to get some rest, but it looks like my mind and my soul had other thoughts because just like that I ended up in Mammon's room. I could feel the breeze caressing my skin and that beautiful smell of grass and water. I could hear the singing of crickets and the wind ruffling the leaves. Everything about nature is majestic all on its own. "You are enjoying the sounds?" The voice startled me a little bit, I knew who it was but for a brief second, I forgot that I was in his room. "Yes, I am, it is a beautiful a sound". "I learned to love that sound myself." "Yamaries why are you here?" he asked sound concerned. "I needed to escape for a little while." "To be honest I just closed my eyes to rest and here I am."

"Where have you been? I was talking to you all the way home and nothing." "I am sorry, I had to think which I am glad you are here. I must go back to hell." "Okay I am going with you." "NO! You cannot go it is dangerous for humans." "I need to save my grandfather's soul." "He should not be in a mason jar in someone's closet waiting to be used." "Mason Jar? What is that?" "Nothing, I can't have him stuck somewhere he doesn't belong, you know that and so do I." "Yamaries if I go to hell, I have to leave your body which means you'll be completely defenseless." "Why can't we go down to together as one?" "Because Yamaries the only way I will be able to go down there is if I fully take over, me being halfway will not cut it down there." "They will see this as weakness and if I am to rule, I must show them that I am the powerful one." "Okay let us do that then, we could play that off good. We have done it before, with your demon powers and some of my angelic power we could be ruthless." "No, I cannot, I must do this alone." "I will follow you to the hole and into hell with or without you knowing, it is your choice." He did not answer right away he just stared at me.

"Okay" he said, "how are we going to tell your grandmother and aunt?" He did have a point, telling my grandmother or aunt that I am leaving with a human guy is bad, but a demon is worse. "I do not know that yet, but we will figure something out." "No Yamaries there is no we, it is just you I do not think you should come with me." "Thanks a lot, I thought we were a team and now you are brushing me off!" "No, I ……" he froze in the middle of that sentence. "I do not know how to explain it as a demon I do not feel, but I care for you tremendously." "I cannot lose you." Wow, I cannot believe he said that I was in all. He said he cared for me. I never thought I will hear that. "I promise if we work together nothing will happen." "We are stronger together; we are a team. We have been through so much together call me selfish, but I cannot lose you." "The thought alone hurts too much." He just stared at me; "do you care for me that much?" "I took over your body without you willing." "I am not good; I am a demon Yamaries, worse I am the prince of Hell." "Not for long" I said, "soon you'll be the King of hell, and to answer your other question, yes Mammon I care so much about you that I am willing to say that I love you and I can't lose you."

Wow, I cannot believe it I am madly in love with my demon. I would have never thought my first real love would be a demon. "We have been through so much together" I told him; "our story does not end with you leaving me behind." He smiled and said, "fine let us go and make new adventures." "Yamaries I must ask you this before we do anything …." before he could finish, I quickly said "yes." "Yamaries, I did not finish my request." He started to laugh I have never seen him laugh before it is nice. "I think I have an Idea what you might want to ask." "Okay then what was I going to ask?" "Can you take full possession over me?" "Yes", he said "that is exactly what I was going to ask you." "Now you know my answer. It is yes, it will always be yes mammon I trust you to the end." He looked surprised and he was speechless, "I never thought I will ever hear any human say that to a demon let alone me." "Well sir, you just did, I give you permission to full take over." He smiled and looked deep into my eyes and said "Yamaries Gonzalez I can finally say this, I never thought that I Mammon would ever find someone that could love me for me and fully embrace it, I finally found my soul mate." "I am in love with you, Yamaries I will love you for all eternity." I am in shock, he said he is in love with me and that I am his soulmate. I leaned closer to him and gave him a kiss and told him "forever and always." He smiled and kissed me. That night I embrace my newfound love for him and his of mine, this and him are my new forever and always.

Chapter Four

The next day, I woke up feeling so good. I have been so confused on my feelings for him, hoping that he will feel the same. I got up from bed, brushed my teeth and went singing down the stairs that is how good I felt. I danced my way to the kitchen, and I did not realize my aunt and grandmother where already in the kitchen. I walked over to the fridge and got startled when I finally realized my aunt and grandmother where at the table smiling. "Good morning", I said with a smile. "you sure are in a great mood this morning", my aunt said. "I am it is a whole new day, with new adventures to conquer". My aunt stopped smiling and gave me a stern look. I quickly recovered and said, "regarding the wedding, you know new adventures". "Oh!' My aunt said and she smiled again. "That is right honey" my grandmother said. "What are we doing first today my beautiful girls?" I smiled from ear to ear, how can I say I am not going to do anything with them. I did have plans with Mammon, but he will have to wait. "We could start by looking for a dress for grandma", I said. "A sexy one to make everyone jealous, and wish they were as beautiful as you". My grandmother smiled and said, "stop playing around Yamaries, pretty dress yes, not sexy I am too old". My aunt looked overjoyed. "So, aunty where do we find the dress". "I have a couple places to go so let us go get ready".

Since I have a couple minutes, I figured I will talk with Mammon and let him know the plans for today. Just like that I was laying in his bed again. I got up and noticed he was not in the room, I jumped off the bed and walked over to the balcony and just stared at the beauty of this place. "Every time you come here you have the same expression as if this were the first time you seen it". "I cannot help it; it is always so beautiful and perfect here". "This place was made for you; its beauty is inspired by yours". Well dang, he got game. He made me blush; and get butterflies in my belly. "What brings you here?" I walked over to him hugged him and just held him. "I just wanted to let you know that I will be shopping with my aunt and grandmother today for the wedding dresses". "Okay", he said "that is good, because you'll have to tell them your goodbyes". "Huh?" I let him go and just stared at him. "I leave for hell as soon as possible I have already sent word". "OH, okay, well that was quick", "it is" he said, "the more I wait the more chaos there will be". "What about your sister?" "I am not sure how much longer she will be able to run hell without one of the demons get out of hand". "Loard is right they will never obey her". "I do not know what or how to tell them." He lifted my face up to look at him directly in the eye and he said, "I will give you two days to see what you come up with". "That will also give me enough time to think of a strategy to get your grandfather". "Getting in is easy, getting him out is completely different". "I understand, I will try to think of something as well". "No, you enjoy your day today and think of something to tell your grandmother and aunt". I smiled, just when I think, you couldn't surprise me you say the sweetest things. He smiled and gave me a kiss. "Now go before your aunt realizes you are not there". "I Love you Mammon" I told him and "I will love you always".

I awoke in my room; I quickly ran into the bathroom and took a shower before the water got cold. The day I spent with my aunt and grandmother was so much fun. We laughed and carried on; I have not seen us this happy in a long time. My aunt was crying because she was laughing so hard, my grandmother making jokes and I am taking it all in. My small family needed to be normal for one day and for that day we were. We went to a restaurant for dinner, and we were having a conversation about my aunt's wedding and my grandmother asked the one question I think every mom would ask when their daughters are going to get married, "so how fast is the baby coming after?" My aunt rolled her eyes and said, "mom do not start that, we are trying to live as a married couple first". I just laughed; we were being way to normal. "We are going to wait two years before we start discussing children", "now aunty you know things do not always go as planned and, in this family, planned stuff never happens". "Great Yamaries thank you know I feel like I am going to get pregnant in less than a year". We all started to laugh; my aunt was being way to dramatic. I see an opportunity to go ahead and make something happen, speaking about futures I said, "since I think we are all in a good place I was thinking about going to college". "That is a great Idea Yamaries" my aunt said, "no more holding off". "I want to set everything straight and normal routines should be picked up and leave the pass behind us where they belong". Well, that went a little better than I thought, okay now for part two.

"We will, my friend from high school is going to a good university in Charlotte I was wondering if I could go visit her on campus to look around see if that is a fit for me". "Of course, with your permission grandma". My grandmother looked at me and said "Yamaries you are eighteen years old; the decision is all yours". "You cannot put your life on hold to make sure everyone is okay". "I am okay, your aunt is way beyond okay she is getting married". "Now you need to go to school get a good degree with a great job that you love meet a nice guy marry him and start your own family". "Make your mom and dad proud, I know that they are looking down at you and see that they did a great job in raising you". I got tearful when she mentions my parents, it always happens. I have not cried like I use to in the beginning it is getting a little easier to handle my crying, it is never getting easy when you lose both your parents. "I think you should go and grab that opportunity". "Thank you, grandma I am going to call her tonight, and I am leaving in two days and I will be gone for two weeks". "Well, that is moving fast do not you think?" I had to think quickly, "well I was already discussing it with her, but I was too afraid to bring it up, with everything going on I didn't want you to think that I was being ugly". My aunt facial expression when from confusion to guilty, "you should never feel that way, you use to talk to me about anything". "Not lately", I told her, "you have been so busy with the wedding and grandma I did not want to add any more stress than I should". My aunt was going to say something, but my grandmother quickly intervenes and said, "see just like her mother so compassionate", "Yamaries?" "Yes grandma?" "What about the demon inside you?" "Is he okay with you taking over and living this life?" "Grandma he going to leave my body and possess someone else". "He is not like any other demon, he is different". "Are you sure?" She said concerned. "Do not fall for his desist, they do that very well". "I will not grandma I am strong just like you". She smiled and said "yes, yes you are".

That night was the best and the last night I had with them like that. For the next two days I placed a smile on my face packed a bag like I was really going somewhere I could use clothes. I took naps and went to bed early one, just so I could be with Mammon and two, so I won't get on their nerves. The easy part like he mentions before was going in but coming out is extremely hard. We must take in mind by that time we have alerted every demon of our presence. On the last day of us strategizing mammon looked at me and said, "to go to hell you are going to have to let go of this body". "Human form is hard to maintain in hell". "How does Zozo do it with my grandfather's body?" "I am sure in intervals". "A human body cannot sub-stain being on the other side." "Where am I going to leave my body?" "There is a place I remember when I possessed someone else that it was safe and secluded." "Okay and then?" I asked, "you will have to die." "What?! Wait?! Huh?!" "Your soul must exit out, that is the only way." "Okay if I die how am I going to go back in the body later?" "That is the hard part" he said, "there is an old spell of my father's that I must find and get." "I heard him talk about it once." "Great two things, we must retrieve?" "Yes, and one more thing." "Oh no what?" "I must show you what I look like again." "Oh of course, I thought it was going to be something serious." "Yamaries this is serious I should have done this a long ago, I was too afraid that you would not feel the same." "Mammon that will not change the way I feel for you. The way I feel for you is already embedded in my heart and soul." "Even so he said I will show you before we go down, because I will look like that down there, I will always look like that." "Go ahead and I will show you that what you look like does not matter and it will never ever change the way I feel." He half smiled and he slowly started to change, it was like nothing I have seen before. Last time he quickly flashed me, now he is gradually changing. It is almost like more a caterpillar changing into a butterfly in the sense of the color change. I do have to admit that I have forgotten what he looked like. I only seen his true form once in the women's bathroom his body and face were burned, his teeth were pointy his fingers were long and his eyes those piercing red eyes. Even with all that it did not bother me at all. His looks do not matter to me, what he feels is all I care about. I went up to him grabbed his face in my hand and gave him a kiss and told him "now there is the man I love." He smiled and said, "now my true love lets go and find your grandfather."

The next morning, I awoke and got myself ready. I grabbed my stuff and walked downstairs. My aunt and grandmother we are already down there making me breakfast and snacks for the road. "Grandma, aunty you do not have to do that I will be there in less than two hours." "Yes, but you will buy junk food the minute you step off the bus, so this is for the ride." "Okay", I did not argue because I knew I was not going to win. "Okay y'all do not miss me too much, I will be home soon." "Do not Flatter yourself Yamaries, you are only going to be gone for two weeks." "Speak for yourself" my grandmother said, "I will miss you my negrita." "Love you grandma", my grandmother gave me some money I told her I had some my parents left me a lot of money and believe it or not they left me the home in Chicago. I thought I lost it forever, but my grandmother and grandfather have been renting it until I was old enough to decide what to do. The Uber got there, and I gave them a hug and jumped into the car. On the ride to the bus station my mind kept going through scenario that might happen down there and how I could get out of it. Mammon and I are going to be in a disadvantage because We cannot merge. Speaking of merging my mind trailed off, I am not sure how I feel about dying. It scares me to know that I am going to die and knowing is the worst part. Before I knew it, I was at the bus station, my mind had wandered for a while. I handed the gentleman the money and walked out. Great, I told myself I was not supposed to go this far. Aww well time to rethink. I knew I could not go back into our town without everyone recognizing me, so I had to stay in the out skirts of town, my grandparents did live in the Boonies. "Okay mammon I need to hail another Uber to the secluded location".

I used my app and got and Uber. Once the Uber arrived, I gave him the address and he took one look at me and said, "you sure?", "Yes" I responded. He turned around and drove to the location. We arrived at a small wooden cabin; it looks nice but looks can be deceiving at times. "Are you sure, you're going to be okay here alone?" the Uber driver asked "Oh, I am not alone all my friends should be arriving soon." "Okay then be careful" Thank you, I said "have a great afternoon." Man, that Uber driver was nosey, sweet though. I stood out by the front door to watch the Uber leave just in case, and because I did not know how to get in. "We really did not think this through Mammon." "Yamaries you should know me a little better than that. Look underneath the mat", "WOW!?" "Why would you place the keys under the mat?" "Because that is where all the human's place's them." "Yeah, in the 50's, now in days you'll get rob that way." We walked into the cabin and it is beautiful, the minute you walk-in there was the living room small but look so cozy. There was even a small fireplace, come to think of it this might be the way to warm up to the house. At the far-right hand side there was the kitchen, to the left a small dining table with four chairs. Next to the dining room there was a door to the room. As I walked closer to the room, I could see another hallway. I walked down the hall and there was a small laundry room and the back door. I looked out the back-door window and there was nothing but trees and woods.

We were far from home, I walked towards the room and I heard a small creaking noise as though someone was walking in the living room. I slow down my walk and stopped right at the threshold between the hallway and the dining room. I peeked to see if I could catch a glimpse of whatever is there, but I could not see anything. I slowly worked my way to the bedroom door, when I reached the doorknob, I heard a laugh coming from behind me. That laugh is so soothing and very intoxicating. Mammon quickly took over and I was no longer in control. I am so glad mammon let me see and hear the conversation. "Loard, thank you for coming back". "Master, I would crawl from the darkest deepest pit of hell for you". "Loard, I summoned you up here to help me because I trust you Loard, do not fail me". His voice was very authoritative, that was very sexy. "Yes, my king you can trust me, I have served your father for millenniums". "I am his confidante and I'll soon be yours". "Thank you Loard, I am going down, but I do not want anyone to know, I might have a target. Especially if Zozo finds out I am down there". "Master, I will not tell a soul". "I know some secret tunnels that can get you into the castle master". Castle! I said to myself, oh, my he lives in a castle. "Good Loard good, one more thing I need this also to stay between us. I am not descending to hell alone". "Master?" "I am bringing someone special to me". Aww! I am his someone special. "Yes, master as you wish, when shall we begin the descent?" "Soon, I am here because first I need to detach from this body and then we must extract her soul". "Master?" Loard said with a little hesitation. "Yes Loard?" "You have fallen for the little human misses? Has she seen your true form, master?" "Yes Loard", Mammon answer "I have fallen for her, and to answer your second question yes, she has seen my true form". "No master your true form?"

Okay, I said to myself now I am intrigued. What does he mean by that? Mammon has shown me his true form twice. "Loard, I have already answered your question, I will not repeat myself". "My apologizes master; it will never happen again". "So, master how are we going to extract her soul?" "Well, I thought we either drown her or these humans now in days like taking these medications that puts you to sleep and they die". "Which, may I add takes the fun out of death". Loard Laughed and it was so intoxicating. "Master there is a family secret, but I can extract the little master's misses from her body". "Oh?" Mammon sounded interested, "How so Loard? how come I have never known of this family secret?" "Dad has always confided in me about our family affairs". "Master your dad Shared what he needed to. I have been here since the beginning". "I know you have Loard therefore I am trusting you". "Yes, master shall we beginning the extraction". "Master?" Loard looked profoundly serious, and he was not playing around, "I give you fair warning, this extraction will be hard on the little master's misses". "In what sense Loard?" "She is going to feel extreme pain, she will scream but master you need not interfere, once the extraction begins you cannot stop it, or she could die". Okay, I thought to myself that sounds extremely dangerous, I think I like Mammon's idea with the pills. "Loard Maybe we should try something different?" "Master?" "I do not want her in pain". I finally spoke up, Loard already knows how much Mammon cares for me so it should not matter if I speak. "No Mammon let this extraction happen". "We do not have time to waste". I expected Loard expression to change but he gave me nothing. No surprise look, no happy look, crap I would have even accepted an angry look. "Yamaries?' Mammon said, "are you sure?" I put on my authority voice on and said "yes, we cannot waste any time. Pills take too long to hit and drowning well let just say I know it is coming". "We need to get started; I have been through far more pain". Loard just looked at me, of course two voices were coming out of one person so he might be confused, I think. "Yes, fine" Mammon said, "let us begin".

Loard bowed his head and said, "as you wish master". That is funny, he would not agree with me, but he would with Mammon. I am not sure if I should be offended or not. Loard walked away and began preparing the area he was going to use. "Yamaries?" Mammon snapped me out of the trance I was in, just knowing that I am going to feel pain scared the crap out of me. "Yes?" I tried to answer quickly. "You do not have to do it this way, we could wait for the pills to do its job". I must be strong I told myself, I need him to see that Mammon might be a demon, but I am a strong woman to have by his side. "No, Mammon I am going to do this, we really do not have time to waste and this is no longer up for discussion." I could hear his smile, and he said, "As you wish". I grabbed my bag and walked into the room to place everything down and my mind could not stop racing and just thinking about the pain. I quickly got my mind back on track, I did not want him thinking I was scared or changing my mind. I walked out of the room and seen the Livingroom was different. I was only in the room for five minutes, so I thought. The Livingroom looked as though we were going to summon a demon. There were no tables, no chairs, and no sofas. I am so used to seeing a pentagram with the five-point star and a circle around the five points but what I saw was completely different.

Yes, there was a circle, and, in the circle, there was one black candle on the top, one white candle on the bottom and two red candles on either side. In between the candles on the floor there was markings, something I have never seen before, it is funny they look somewhat tribal. The lights where dim, it looked somewhat eerie. I looked around and did not see Loard anywhere. I kept looking around the room and noticed three tables that were filled with water, "that is odd" I said. "Yes, it is, my master use's water as a conduct." That Voice it was so soothing, "Loard? Where were you?" I managed to ask him. I am here there and everywhere I looked around and finally caught his face in front of me, his head tilted every time he said something as though he was trying to hypnotize me. "Little miss shall we begin?" Everything I felt was gone, things started to look weird, and the room seemed out of focus. "Little Miss, I have relaxed you; I cannot have you ruining the spell and hurting my master". "Huh?" I was so confused; did he just drug me? How did he have time? When? I could see him walking closer to me, but I could not move. He grabbed my hand and walked me over to the circle. I felt drunk, yes, I do know what that felt like. I was not always a know it all. I walked into the circle and laid down. My feet where close together, my arms spread out. My Fingertips on each hand touched the red candles. Both my big toes touched the white and the black candle touched the top of my head. Now it made sense the tribal writing was like a small circle around me. "Little miss? Are you comfortable?" "Yes", I said, I knew I was in a Trans everything seems so fuzzy, I was answering without knowing. I hated that feeling, "let us begin". Loard moved his hands and the tables moved. I am not sure why, but I tried to move. It could be one of my instinct of fright and flight, but I could not move, it felt like something was holding me down. I wanted to panic but I could not, I have lost all control of myself. "Now, now little miss you do not want to feel the pressure of my circle". With a wave of his hand, a cup of water lifted from the table and poured over my feet. another wave of his hand and another cup of water poured on my hand. The cups of water kept poured on me, my body was soaked. "Now little misses just relax", every time he said that I feel deeper into a Trans.

He did something different as he waved his hand, he said "Lomous Unos", the cup flew up over my head and the water poured over my face. I started to panic a little, but I could not move. "Now little misses you know better", Loard said, he snapped his fingers and said "Nious, Unos" his eyes turned bright purple and the big circle caught fire. I was completely wet, and I could not wipe my face, I had some water up my nose, it was painful. Loard raised his hands up, the candles lite up, his eyes changed from bright purple to a bright blue, and he began his incantation. With his hands still up over the circle he said "Uforia, Tunos, Minus" with that I felt my body start to burn a little, like a heat running through my veins, not painful but more uncomfortable.

I still could not move I wanted to be able at least shift. "Inferno, Umos, Nuasos" The burning began to get stronger, and I started to feel pain. The burning was so intense I wanted to rip my skin off; it was coursing through my veins. "Unos Eterno Mortares" he kept chanting and his eyes began to change color once more, this time they changed into a bright red. The pain was unbearable, I started screaming so I thought but there was no sound. The pain was so bad at this point I could not even concentrate on what Loard was doing. "Lorutas, Encanto, Inferneto" He yelled this last incantation, and he lifted his hands, it literally felt like my heart ripped from my chest. Everything went black; I could not see or hear anything.

I slowly started to come to, I opened my eyes and at first, everything was blurry. I blinked a couple times and things were starting to clear up. I felt funny almost as if I were floating. I Brushed it off I figured it had to do with the spell. I did notice that it was nighttime, I wonder how long I was out. I started to sit up slowly; I still felt a little dizzy. I was able to get myself together and looked around, "Loard?" I spoke. "Mammon?" I wonder if it worked. I hope it did because I cannot go through that again. Nobody answered I started to get a little worried. I got this surge of anger; they better have not left me here. "Little master's misses are you okay?" His voice sounded different, it was not soothing or memorizing as it used to be, it was normal. Huh? That is odd I wonder what changed. "Yes, Loard everything is okay, did it work?" I said with a smile. "Yamaries?" His voice sounded so sexy; I knew exactly who that was. I turned my head, and I could not believe what I saw.

It was as if he was in slow motion. The most beautiful man I have ever since, I swear for a little I thought I seen a light glowing around him. He smiled big, it was probably because my mouth was open and yes, I think I drooled a little bit. "Mammon?" Was the only thing that came out, why me? "I am confused" I said, "you do not need to hide'. "You are handsome in your true form as well; you do not need to hide from me anymore". He shook his head and smiled; "this is how I know you are the one". "You do not care what I really look like, Yamaries I am sorry I lied to you, but this is my true form". "Huh?" I said I am confused "I thought…" I could not even finish my sentence. He said, "I am half angel and half demon'. Everyone seems to forget that my dad Lucifer is an angel; he is not grotesque with horns. I inherited his looks". "My sister on the other hand she inherited my mother's looks". He made me laugh; I quickly got up and started to walk to him to give him a hug. I was glad it worked; I stopped in my tracks when I see that his smiled was gone. "What?" I asked him, he made me nervous. "Yamaries, how are you feeling?" "I am okay, I feel great. Mammon what is going on?" "Yamaries you are dead". I was confused because I could feel my legs and my arms, I was standing up right and was able to walk simply fine. "No, Mammon I think you are confused", Mammon walked over to me stopped me from moving back and forth. He turned me around to where I was laying and I could not believe what I saw, it was me.

I placed my hands over my mouth and said, "oh my god, Mammon that is my body?" "Yes", he responded, "the reason it hurt so much was because it was not only a detachment from me, but it was also killing you in the process". "Let me explain, if your heart stops there is nothing more for me to hold on to. Your soul or the person's soul would give into me and let go. In your case we forced you to let go". WOW! I cannot believe this, "why didn't you just tell me?" 'I would have still gone through with it'. "I did not realize what was happening until it was done". "I felt everything you were feeling from the pain to the restraint, I was also helpless at that point". "I am so sorry Yamaries, something like this will never happen again". I felt so betrayed and angry, especially at Loard, why did he think I would not go through with it? I didn't show how upset I was because in reality if I knew how much pain it would have been or known that I was going to die I think I might have no went through with it, so I'll just let this one slid. "No, No I am not upset, what is done is done let keep move on". Mammon turned to Loard and said, "Do not let this ever happen again because rest a shore there will not be another chance". "I am sorry master, but this had to be done, if little miss were not true, she would have not with you". "Her soul and body would be soul would have both been gone". "Loard!!" Mammon voice roared with rage, "I do the testing around here you do not", "DO I MAKE MYSELF PERFECTLY CLEAR!!" His eyes turned bright red. "Yes master", Loard bowed his head turned over to me and said, "I apologize little miss". "Mammon do not…" He gave me a glare as if do not do that. It was a little scary to see those red eyes, but I stood my ground. "Mammon do not get mad at him; he cares for you and for your family this is his way of making sure his family stays safe". "We humans do that as well, so do not be too hard on him okay". I turned to Loard and said, "Well Loard as you can see, I am true, I will never hurt you or your family". "Now gentleman" I said with an upbeat tone, I was tiring to lighten up the room because it was getting way too intense for me. "Let us get pass this and get to work". "Shall we start heading to the portal so we could make our descent? Loard please lead the way", Loard bowed his head and said, "yes little miss".

Loard began to walk to the door, and I grabbed mammon and said, "sometimes you need to pick and choose your battles, this was not one, he was only trying to help." "I know it might not have looked that way, but he really does care for you." Mammon looked at me and said, "not with you, he could play with my soul all he wants but when it comes to you, I will kill him first." He pulled away and headed out the door, he really is stubborn. I walked towards the doorway and the strangest thing happened, I got these flashes it was very disorienting at first, but then it became easier to tolerate. a bright flash of light shinned right in my face and within this light there was an outline of a man, a man with wings. "What!? Was that?" Is that what I think it might have been. Was that and angel? And just like that he was gone. "Yamaries!" I ran out the door and Mammon looked confused and a little worried. "Are you okay?" I did not want him to worry so I lied, "yeah, I have to get use to this. It feels funny now that I know I am just a spirit". Loard was looking at me like he knew I was lying. "Master, shall we continue?" I really do need to stop assuming things. "Yes, Loard let us proceed" Mammon said, we started heading towards the woods. "Mammon where are we going exactly?" I asked a little confused, I am not sure why I asked that question I should have remembered that question, but Mammon answered anyway. "Well, we are going to hell do you not remember?" "Funny, funny Mammon you do know the portal is back where I live". "Yes, I do know that there is one by your home, but we are not going that way that could alert them of our presence". "I am trying to get us at least to my home and then maybe we could set the alarm". Well doesn't he have jokes today, "Okay I just forgot, I did not know that there is an alarm we could trigger when you enter the portal." "Well, you are right there is an alarm that does go off once someone steps through the portal, see portal are made by magic and certain incantations have what you call, and alarm set by the one who congers it just alerting them". "Well, that is good to know, okay so are we creating a portal?" "No, we do not have to create a portal because the place Loard is going to take us through is old and has been open for a long time." "I am sorry I haven't kept you up to speed on what the plans are", I quickly felt guilty because I know I am keeping something from him, and he is here letting me know everything.

I still am not going to tell him anything regarding what I saw. I do not think right now is the right time, I never thought that angels would exist, but Demons exist why not angels. I can say that I never thought in my wildest dream that I would encounter one. I was in deep concentration when I heard some leaves crack and wood breaking. "Yamaries?" Mammon said cautiously, "Yes Mammon I heard that." We were all frozen in our spot looking around for an attack. "Mammon you did say that nobody knows we are out here, right." "Well, that is true but now I am not sure." Once again, I heard ruffling of the leaves on my right side. "Loard, are you able to see anything?" Mammon asked. "No, master but I am going to draw out Demonus, my sword." "No Loard wait, we do not want to scare a human". "Mammon humans cannot see us, right?" "Well, the sensitive ones can". We looked around and we couldn't see anything, and the noise stopped. "how much of a walk do we have left?" "Not much little miss, we should be getting there within five miles". "Five miles huh?" Does he think that is a short period of time. "Now if someone or something is following us little miss then we might have to change locations". Right when Loard finish his sentence there was a snap of a branch. Then something shot up from the trees breaking branches on the way up, I am not sure, but I think I seen wings. "What can that be?" "Whatever that thing is, it sounds big and strong". "Mammon please tell me that you could see what that is, I think it has wings." Loard answered before mammon did, "Something us demons would not want to encounter. Master I think it might be gone". This is starting to get too intense for me, I told myself. We started to walk again and finally got to our location. I swear things just got creepy, I thought we arrived at a place in a horror movie when things go horrible. After we went through the trees and bushes, we came across this opening where right in the middle there was an abandoned house.

There was nothing else surrounding this house but trees. The house looked like it was falling apart, one wrong move and I think the whole building would collapse. I could see on the right of me that there was a driveway, or something that was supposed to be a driveway. I really had to work hard in seen a certain distance because I was in complete darkness. I was lucky enough to see the house and my hands, we began to walk closer to the house, and I swear I thought someone was looking at us. As we got to the front door of the house, I began to experience this pain, it was horrible it was if my veins were on fire. I stopped in my tracks and called out to Mammon. "Mammon, I am in pain, what is this?" Loard answered, "this will go away little miss, it is your first time." "You will see soon enough why you hurt so bad". Mammon looked over at Loard and he looked annoyed, "Next time let me answer, she was directing her question to me". "I am sorry master it will never happen again". "Shall we go inside and get the portal open?" "Yes", I responded I looked over at Mammon and said, "it is starting to subside". "I am sorry for keeping you out here to long", "do not apologize little miss, this is not your fault". "Let us go inside", I could feel someone staring at me, the feeling got so strong I was afraid to look back, but I did anyways. As I turned around, I was in shock by what I saw. "What the..." I could not finish my sentence. Was I seeing this correctly?

Chapter Five

I could see people walking around, I know they were not there a little while ago. I looked closer and notice these people were not alive they were dead. Some of the people had modern clothes some had eighteen century clothes, some had gunshot wounds to the head, well and some looked as though they have been tortured. "Umm, am I the only one that can see this?" Mammon looked at me and said, "no Loard and I can also them." "I know everything that is going to start happening to you is going to be new, but rest assure that Loard and I will be able to see and feel everything you do". "This will take some time, but you will get used to it". I do not think that I am going to be able to get use to this. "Come Yamaries let us go inside, we have much work to do before we begin our journey". I could not stop staring at them, I felt so bad that they were roaming around here on earth with no peace. From the corner of my eye, I seen a black shadow go from left to right, but this thing was fast. I turned quickly to look but I could not see anything. I turned to look at Mammon and Loard to see if they saw what I just did but, they were concentrating on something else. I turned back around and started to look around, I didn't notice myself-doing this, must have been an instinct or just plain stupidity but I started to walk down the stairs and into the middle of the front yard. I walked far enough that I could see the roof of the house. There it was hovering on top of the roof straight at me. I could not move or scream it was as if I lost all functions of my body. This thing hovering over the house had wings coming from his back, he was half human. His wings were black, and he had the most piercing eyes. He was almost angelic as the moon light shined on him, those eyes red as fire with some blue as the sky, it was intimidating. I am not sure what made Loard turn to look at me, but he yelled "little miss is everything okay?" "Why are you in the middle of the field?" I could not respond all I did was start to tear up, once I heard mammon my tears were at full flow falling off my face and onto my chest. "Yamaries what is wrong? I know that look". Loard and Mammon came running towards me but the minute they were visible to whatever that was over on the roof, it was gone. Mammon was the first one to get to me and held me and said, "Yamaries what is wrong?" I finally said something, "Mammon there was someone on the roof, he was scary and very intimidating and Mammon he had wings". Loard looked at mammon and gave this weird look and Mammon grabbed my face and said, "okay listen to me carefully, Yamaries what can you remember from what you saw? I need details". Okay that is weird, but I guess I will have to try and remember. That was the strangest thing I could not remember what exactly I saw, all I could remember was he had wings. "I cannot remember I just know he had wings"; I felt a little uneasy about that. How can I not remember what I just finish seeing? that scared me. "What color was his wings Yamaries?" "What color was his eyes?" "Was it he or she?" "Mammon please stop asking me all these questions I cannot remember". I began to cry why cannot I remember. "I just remember he has wings and yes, it is a guy". I looked over at the house and seen something in the window and would not you believe it had wings. "Mammon, Loard!!!" I hollered "he is in the house on the second floor!" They left my side and Loard went inside the house and Mammon went around the side of the house. They were not playing around, they know something I didn't, but what could it be.

I finally got myself together and realized I was in the middle of the field with a lot of dead people walking around and shadows poking their heads out occasionally from behind the trees, it was scary. I also could not help but feel bad, my emotions were everywhere. I wonder what they are feeling, those poor souls. I am a soul; I keep forgetting that I am going to be like them one day. I was in deep thought with my feelings when I decided to pan around and look at the different face of the dead, and like a flash I seen those eyes. I got so scared I pushed back a little and closed my eyes, I know I am dead, but I swear I thought I could feel my heart beating so fast. I felt each pulse through my neck, and I began controlling my breathing. I took two deep breathes and opened my eyes again, and it was gone. I could not see anything but the dead, I started panning around again a little more frantic and I did not see it again. I decided to go in a circle and look behind me because of course that is what dumb people do, I did a turn, and nobody was behind me except the dead but once I turned back to face the house all I seen was those red and blue eyes. I will tell you what, if I had all body functions I would have crapped and peed my pants right there. I was in complete panic, paralyzing state and there was nothing I could do about it. His head kept going side to side looking at me, inspecting every inch, "Yamaries" it said. "Such a beautiful girl", his voice was so relaxing, and it almost sounds like music. "Do not be afraid" he continued, he got closer and smelled me, nope that was not creepy at all, I thought to myself. I know I thought that him smelling me was creepy, but I couldn't help but smell him since he was so close. He smelled like cookies, I could not explain it, he smelled sweet and just like that I was not afraid of him anymore. "I remember that scent" he kept going, he ran his finger down my face and said, "it is so familiar to me, but I cannot really place it". I heard Mammon and Loard coming, they were having a conversation and he turned around to look at them and said, "my sweet Yamaries this conversation will have to wait for another time, until we meet again". Just like that he was gone, I dropped to the ground and began to cry for no reason. I was not scared, sad or hurt, I was just. I heard Mammon yell "Yamaries!!" I am coming" and he ran my way as fast as he could. I couldn't explain it but I felt like I had no emotions but was expressing all of them, Once mammon reached me is when I snapped out of whatever I was in and I screamed so loud I think I actually scared the dead. Mammon held me and I began to cry, "Yamaries what happened?" I could not answer him I felt like I lost my voice. I just stared at him and he said, "that is okay Yamaries lets go inside", "Loard go open the front door we are going to take her inside". "Yes, master as you wish, I will get started on the portal". Loard started heading to the house and mammon picked me up and carried me to the house. I felt so helpless week and I felt like I was so much trouble for Mammon and Loard. I felt like they needed to watch me all the time. I just held him close and sobbed on his neck, we reached the house and finally went inside. Mammon placed me on the ground and said can you walk? "Yes, thank you". Mammon smiled and said to have a seat in the living room and get some rest I am going to see if Loard needs my help. I could not believe it, the house had full power and the lights were on, this house looks nothing like the outside. The house was emasculate, once you walk in on the left side was the living room, it was big. There was a fireplace two couches and a small table in between the couches. On the right was the dining room. The table that was there sat at least ten people four on each side and one at the end and head of the table. Mammon walked into the living room, walked over to me and said "Yamaries, are you okay?" "No, mammon I am not, I am not sure who that was, but he knew who I was". "It was as if he had a hold on me, but I was not afraid, i felt so comfortable that if he would ask me to do anything I would". "I am sorry I was not there to protect you; I should have known that was a bad Idea". "Do not be sorry Mammon, you did not know shoot I did not know". I looked into mammon's eyes and just stared, "Yamaries what is it?" "There something about your eyes that remind me of his". As fast as it came to me, it was gone.

"Yamaries what do you mean?" Mammon looked very curious and wanted to know more about it, but I could remember much anymore of him or what he looked like. "Oh umm, I am not sure I thought I saw something, but it is gone now". "Master, the portal is ready", Loard came in just in time. "Shall we begin our descent?" "Yes", Mammon said with a little bit of hesitation, "but we need to move fast I think something might be on to us". Mammon Looked at Loard and gave him a look that only they could understand because Loard quickly moved towards the front door and checked out to see if there was something there. "Okay Mammon am I missing something here?" "No, we are just being extra careful". Loard came back inside and said, "Let us go master", and that was the end of that weird conversation with vague words. Mammon and I got up and headed outside towards the portal, there it was a big purple lighted portal and as you walk closer to it you could see stairs.

Once I got to the portal, I knew there was no turning back after that, I took a deep breath and I walked through the portal. After Loard walked through the portal, it closed behind him, we slowly began our descent down those narrow stairs that look like they might give out. I looked around at my surrounding and I could not believe it I think we might be in a cave. I started to smell fresh dirt; it was not a bad smelling at all it was almost sweet. It felt as the steps were never ending, I thought we were never going to stop going down, this took descending to a whole other category. Just when I was about to complain I noticed that we were coming up on an opening, Loard looked at me and said, "I will enter first little miss you second and then the master". I knotted in agreeance, The opening was dark and very scary looking I hesitated a little before I walked through, I gave myself a pep talk and said why are you so afraid nothing can be scarier than what you have already been through. I pulled myself together and walked through as I walked through, I felt a small electrical pulse go through me. It was the weirdest feeling, but all that was taken away once I seen what I walked into. This place was gorgeous We were inside the mason, I told mammon "were we not just in a cave?" He smiled and said, "nothing down here is as it seems" and he walked away. Now that was hot, I must admit he sometimes has those movie man qualities. "Yamaries, Welcome to my home". His home was beautiful and huge, the walls were red with black designs. I really could not make out the design, but it was beautiful non the less. The ceiling was high cathedral style, and the doorways where mid-evil. There were mirrors and art. The furniture looked awfully expensive and where goth style it was so luxurious, impressive design of black and red embroidery of LM initials. LM, I said to myself, Lucifer Morningstar, Conceited much. Everything in the home flowed perfectly together, I could not believe how mystical everything was. I finally got myself out of the trance and looked at Mammon who was smiling away at me. "Do you like what you see?" He almost sounded as if he wanted to laugh at me, I wonder if my mouth was open the whole time I was staring at his house. "Yes, it is beautiful, why ask that question?" "Well your mouth was open the whole time you were staring and your eyes where a little shiny". Great, I knew it. "Ha-ha, you have jokes I see, your home is beautiful". "Come let me show you the rest of the house". I looked at Mammon and said "I am so glad you want to show me around and please don't take this wrong because I am very nosey and I want to go explore your home but shouldn't we be figuring out what to do next and how where going to get my grandfather?" "Yes, I do, do you know where he is at? because I do not, that is why I sent Loard on a mission to go figure out places where Zozo might be hiding". "Wherever he is at I am sure that your grandfather will be there, we never leave our prize possession behind". "What I do need to look for is the spell to be able to release your grandfather and while I am looking for that I can show you around". Well he had all of that planned, I felt dumb, "thank you so much for doing this, you did not have to". "Yes, you are right I did not", oh hell no did he just agree with me, "but Yamaries", he said "I wanted to do this". Oh well damn well played, "now", he said "let show you to your room". My room? I did not know I had a room down here. You know for a half demon and half angel he sure is modest. "Okay then let us go and have a looksie shall we", I said with a smile. Every hallway we went through was just as beautiful as the last. We finally reach the hallway to go up the stairs and I really should not be this amazed but there were spiral stairs. I did not even know they could make them this big, I always pictured them small and narrow. This was grand and elegant; I was speechless once again. We walked up the stairs and finally made it to the top where there was a long hallway, we walked all the way to the end and my room was the one on the left. That is funny it is almost like my grandparents' house, we walked into the room and I was in all, there was a grand fireplace. There was a beautiful wood design that bordered along the fireplace. A gothic four pillar king size bed in black with red sheets. A beautiful black throw rug, red slippers on it. Can you believe there is a double door balcony opening? Oh my, he has been in my head. I looked around in all, "do you like the room?" I turned to him and said "Are you kidding me? I am in love". He smiled "I am glad to hear that. Now relax change and meet me downstairs in the great hall. We have to strategies and see if we have leads". "Oh, and Yamaries?" "Yes, I know do not take too long". "No stay away from the windows and that balcony, for two reasons one nobody knows we are here and two you are not yet ready to handle what is out there". Okay I said to myself that was dark, "oh okay I promise I will not". Mammon walked out of the room and closed the door behind him. I tip toed to the door to hear if he was gone. "OMG! This house is amazing!" I yelled as I twirled around the room. Yes, you heard correctly I twirled. Once I got myself together, I thought about something, Can I take a shower I am dead, do we shower? Oh, and what am I going to change into? I walked over to the closest and opened it, this closet was huge, and it had clothes in it already. I looked at the size of the clothes and they were my size, now that is creepy. I ignored it and closed the door and went to go take a shower, even if I am a spirit, I am still going to be a clean one it my instincts. I got in the shower and turned on the water can you believe it I feel the water hitting me as if I had skin. It is as if I never died at all. Once I was done taking a shower I got out and was going to head over to the closest to get some clothes but noticed that there were clothes already on the bed for me. I walked over to it and there was a red shirt and black pants. The pants looked skintight, how am I going to get into those? Wait where these clothes already out? Or did he come back while I was in the shower? I have questions. I looked at the pants again and said out loud "I hate Crotch huggers", whatever I guess I will wear them I do not want to go looking for other pants. I quickly got dressed and started to head downstairs, as I was approaching the bottom of the steps, I could hear a conversation going on.

"No, we must find another way to get through, I am not going to let her go through there". I felt a little rude just listening, so I quickly jumped into the conversation while I had the chance, "Go through what?" Mammon and Loard stopped their conversation and looked at me, but neither one of them answered me. "Loard" I said, "what is going on". "Yamaries", mammon said as if he was caught sticking his hand in the cookie jar. "Loard was giving me information on the where about of your grandfather". "That is great news", I could contain my excitement. "That was quick", I said, "Yamaries please do not bring your hopes up, I said that this might be the location where he is at, I never said he was there". I looked at mammon and said, "that is good enough for me". "Where is it?" "That is just its" Mammon said, "where they think he is at is extremely dangerous to go, I need to make sure he is there before we head there".

"Well, well if it is not my big bother, the King". "Yvi welcome home", I turned around and there she was Yvi, she was more demon than angel. She was tall with medium size horn; she had a black rash going down her body. She had one eye black and red, the other eye red with black. Her hands and fingers were long, she was very intimating. "Brother who is this?" She said with this stand-offish voice. "Yvi this is Yamaries, she is the one I have been looking for". "Oh, brother of mine you really are helpless, no one could love us". "Dad let us know this when we were young. We are not loveable material", she turned to me and said, "Girly please stop lying to my brother and now I must dispose of you". "It is not personally, oh wait yes, it is". "Yvi, NO!" Loard yelled. Oh no he didn't, Loard just yelled at one of his masters, this is not going to end well. "Loard?! You have the audacity to yell at me, your master". "I am sorry princess, but the little misses has proven herself, she really does love the prince". "Well, it looks like you deceived two demons, your stronger than you look, this is going to be fun". She smiled and her pointed teeth had blood dripping out of them that scared the crap out of me. She raised her hand and the table began to shake. "Umm, mammon what is going on?" "Just stay behind me", he stated, "okay", "I have done that without you having to ask me". "Why is she getting like this?" "You must understand our childhood was as bad as you could think. My sister and I we grew up quite different". Yvi flipped her hand, and the table went flying across the room. Loard tried to intervene with no success. "Loard! you dare come between me and this human girl". "She is Lying to you both! Mammon dad always said you were stronger than me can't you tell". "Yvi stop this right now! I love her and she loves me as well". Yvi screamed and it was this loud ear blowing scream. As she screamed all the glasses in the house popped. Finally, the scream starts to die out and the glass finished hitting the floor as the windows stopped sliding off, at first it was low and distorted, but slowly it made itself very intensifying. There were voices, voices in so much pain, these voices I knew exactly what they were, they were souls. Souls of people who had done bad and now they are being tormented and tortured. These voices at first did not bother me which made me question myself. Then it became unbearable, I could feel their pain, I could not help but feel sorry as they cried for mercy. Mammon Grabbed me and looked into my eyes and said, "Do not feel sorry for these souls, they are bad very bad souls that are living out their worst fears repeatedly as punishment for what they have done on earth". "She will never love you brother; she is merely a human. Humans are selfish, self-centered, and greedy". "Yvi listen to what I am going to say and listen well". Mammon was furious I could see how his eyes turned bright red, is voice when he spoke shook the room, I could feel it in my core he meant business. "If you touch one hair on her head, I will destroy your very core and you will be locked in the dungeon of despair for all eternity. Do I make myself clear!" Yvi's eyes got big, and she backed up a little bit and said, "yes, your majesty whatever you wish". What the actual Fuck! That was insane, really majesty? Was that a battle of power over the throne? Well if it was Yvi lost. "Now sister understand this, I am here to rule in dad's place, no one knows yet, but if anyone finds out I will know it was you and I will not hesitate to punish you". "Yes, your majesty", "and Yvi" Mammon said, "Stop calling me that you know that royalty never calls another royal majesty. You're trying to get under my skin", "is it working" she said. Mammon roared, "alright already calm down brother". If this is a sibling fight, I am glad I never had any, I said to myself. "It is not easy being your twin sister and please do not forget that". TWINS! He never said anything about being a twin. "Yvi Fix and clean things up in here you made an unnecessary mess". "Yamaries, Loard come with me into the grand hall and finish our discussion". I am not sure if Mammon did not trust his sister or if he is upset about the situation, but I thought twins had this unspoken bond to one another.

I pushed that topic to the side and said, "okay" and Loard answered "as you wish master". As I was walking out the room, I could feel her staring at me, I turned around and looked at her, which may I add was a big mistake, those piercing eyes where so intense. Why is she looking at me like that? I did not say anything to her and kept walking. I finally got away from her eyesight and I started to feel better, Loard was waiting for me, "little master's misses are you okay?" "Um, yes Loard I am fine". "Come on little miss its over here". "Um Loard?" "Yes, little miss?" "I want to thank you for having my back, over there. I know that was not easy for you, going against you master". "Now, now little misses no need for all of whatever you are doing, that is my job". Hmm, I wonder if he knows what gratitude is, by the sound of it he has no Idea what I am doing. "Loard I am serious, Thank you". Loard just kept looking at me as if he were ready for me to say Just kidding. I felt bad, he has never had anyone show him how grateful they are. He tilted his head and looked me in the eyes and said, "you're welcome little miss", I smiled and followed him to the grand hall. "Okay, Loard", Mammon said as we walked in, he did not even let me look around. "Do you absolutely know that he is there?" "Master, I would never tell you anything that I don't one hundred percent know it to be true, but master if you like I will go ahead and start heading out and looking around, I'll be back to let you know I also don't want to place the little misses in danger". Just like that Loard walked away, "Humm that is different Loard has never been willing to place his life on the line for anyone". He looked at me and smiled "you must have made an impression on him", I smiled at him and said, "yeah maybe". "Mammon what is it that has you acting this way, in the sense of you getting more intel is it really that dangerous?" "Yamaries you are in my world, things here are not as simple as living on earth. Every step I take here is a good strategy I am going to need you to follow every step that I take with no arguments do you understand?" Oh, there he is the Mammon I know so well, "Yes, I understand" I replied. "There is thing that do go bump in the night and yes everywhere you turn there is going to be something watching you. When you feel those things, you need to inform me. Loard and I will investigate it and take precaution". Well darn he is scaring me, if he does not want me to go, he really is achieving is goal.

"No more talk until Loard comes back, come let me show you something". Really, now I am afraid to move where the hell is he is taking me. "Okay", I said, as I tried to clear my head of all this information. I followed Mammon into the hall, I could not get over how beautiful this house is. Every time I walk into another room, I am in all. He walked me over to a room all the way in the back like a study but before we could get to the study, we had to go through this hallway that was made entirely up of glass. It was insane, it is like we went outside to go to the study, but we never left the house. What I saw was amazing, there where lights, little houses and "oh shit" I hollered "they could see us!" Mammon laughed "no they cannot you could see them, but they cannot see you". "Oh sorry, I did not mean to overreact". "Come along Yamaries this way". After I got my crap together, I realized that it is a community down here, a society just like up on earth, I cannot believe it. I always thought that it would be either cold or hot and dry but always in Chaos.

Nothing was able to thrive, but I was wrong, these demons have their own things going on down here. "Yamaries?" Mammon called out to me. I did not realize that I was still standing in the same spot looking out. I looked over at him, "Huh?" "Oh yeah, I am sorry" I started walking over to him. "It is not as you were told, huh?" Mammon asked me not surprised. "No, it is not", "the stories of hell and the deep emptiness. There are demons down here scary ones, but they are people like up on earth living their lives it is incredible". I looked at him and said, "Nothing is as it seems huh" and I smiled. He smiled at me and said, "come along, I still have something to show you". We finally got to the study and this room, well let me just jump right into it. It had a tall ceiling, black bookshelves that were built from the ceiling to the floor and it was filled with books. The desk was right in front of a big fireplace, the fireplace was decorated with red dragons. The desk was burgundy big and wouldn't you know there was black carpet around the desk. The chair was a throne, oh someone was filling that way too much. Mammon walked over to a wall and said, "you ready?" "Huh?" I said looking very confused. He smiled and hit a code into a panel on the wall and it began to open. Of course, I got a little nervous I didn't know what was going to come through, but to my surprise it was a pool within a cave that has glass windows looking into the city. "What is going on? My eyes are playing tricks on me". He smiled and said, "what you thought us demons cannot have fun? Oh, I see you thought we were mindless and boring". "This is…. I mean…. What..." for the first time in a long time I was speechless. "This is beautiful Mammon". "I swam a lot when I was younger, believe it or not it is boring living down here". "My sister fit in a little bit better than I ever had, but she and I were never twin close like humans are. She and I never see eye to eye, but we do believe in family".

"You know Mammon ...." "Shhh", he said quickly "someone is listening", he came closer to me and pulled me closer, "do you hear that?" "No, I cannot hear anything" I said but I could not hear anything because I could not stop staring at him. He quickly snapped me out of it "Yamaries listen closely". I closed my eyes and I faintly hear breathing, I opened my eyes and said, "someone is breathing". Now without trying I could hear it getting louder as if it were getting closer to us. Then came the scratches on the wall, I was so concentrated on the breathing and the scratching that when the loud laugh came, I jumped.

"I thought I heard it all, my big brother wanting a family of his own", she laughed again. "You always were the funny one", "Yvi what do you want?" Mammon asked. "Stop protecting that human, she will never be able to love because she is human, now a demon she will be able to love you as you deserve, and you know this". Why this bitch, no she is not doing this crap again. Mammon was going to speak but I cut him off, I pulled away from him and said, "look chick I don't know what you're trying to gain here but I am in love with your brother, and no one is going to change that. I am sorry that you only see me as a human but just because a human broke your heart does not mean we are all the same. So, back off before you piss me off even more". Once I said that and really thought about it, I really should not have said that. She is going to kill me. Mammon smiled grabbed my shoulder in agreeance and stood by my side. Yvi's eyes where burning with rage. If looks could kill, I would be lifeless. "Mammon are you going to let this mere human speak to me, royalty this way". "Now, you have done it little girl my brother is going to ..." "Do absolutely nothing Yvi, your brother will do nothing to his future bride". Huh? Wait what? I was all over the place. "You would not dare", Yvi said to mammon, "Yvi why can't I love someone and marry them?" "Brother father will be furious with you. He hates humans and you know this". "I really do not care what he thinks or want, I make my own decisions so back off". These two sounds like spoil kids with daddy issues. Yvi's face calmed down a little, "what is so special about this one that has you acting in such away". "She loves me in return", Mammon said. The look on her face when he said that turned into sadness, "I fear brother that I will never know that feeling, that powerful spell that has you defining our father's rule". She lowered her head and walked away; I could not help but feel sorry. Mammon just stared at her and he looked like he did not even care. "Yvi, I called out wait can I speak with you for a little bit please?" Mammon grabbed my arm and tried to pull me back, I held his hand and said, "it is going to be okay, I promise". Mammon eyes looked worried, so he does have some feelings. He reluctantly let me go and I walked over to his sister who still has not responded to me or smiled in agreement. I was not afraid though I think she needs to be that strong because she must be with these guys and showing them who is boss. I got up to her and she just stared at me, I do not know why or where I got all these nerves from, but I did. "Can we go talk or would you like me to leave you alone?" She had mixed look of confusion and anger. She just stared at me and finally she nodded her head in agreeance. "Follow me", she said that made me a little nervous, but I was the one who initiated this little heart to heart. I followed her through the glass hallway and back into the main house and into the Livingroom. There were two big chairs in front of this beautiful fireplace that was on and ready for someone to sit in front of it and be cozy. I walked over to the chair and sat down, she was walking over to the other chair slowly, I wonder what she thought I was going to do to her. She finally sat down, but she did not look at me she just stared at the fire. I was going to begin but before I could she began. "I do not despise humans just to let you know. She did not look my way at all, I was going to respond to her comment but once again she began her point. "Being raised with my father was not a walk in the park for my brother and me". "Yvi, I said before she decided to jump in, I am not here to judge you or get into an argument with you about your bother, I want to speak with you so you could hear how much I love your brother". "I know I am human-ish, I do not have a body, but we humans are all different. I will not lie to you at first, I hated your brother for tricking me into letting him possess me, but he grew on me". It was a process and I looked passed his rough exterior and found the soft beauty that is your brother". "Yvi, I turned to her and asked her, I need you to look me in the eyes and see my truth". "I love your brother for all his rough edges and his soft side as well, I could only think and act clearly around him, I only see him and me together no one else". She was still looking at me and she said, "what you and my brother have is something I have never seen before, maybe I am jealous or curious". "My brother and I never had a relationship, my father never accepted that", "he was being groomed to be king, while I was being trained to be a warrior and protect my brother", "so our paths barley crossed". "Then, to my surprise, I'd watched my brother living a life different from what I was and that infuriated me". "I wanted that, I did not want to be a warrior, I wanted to rule". "My brother getting all the attention from dad and being groomed to be King, and he throws it all away". "I just do not understand why? All I want to know is why?" "Then I hear you speak about my brother; and here you are, speaking of my brother, I think I am understanding why he is doing the things he does or will do". "Please do not miss understand, I am not okay with it, but I understand". I really did not know how to take that, but I respected her. "Why don't you come and listen to what your brother and I are talking about?" "No", she said very stern, "I do not want an invitation of pity from you". "I did not share my story with you for pity". "If my brother would like me to help or opinion, he will ask me himself". That little snooty shit just pissed me off, I looked at her rolled my eyes and said, "whatever". This chick is nuts, this point after I will not be nice to her, "I am not using your story as a pity story I could care less but I was extending a hand". "Now, I do not care if your brother asks you or not, I will leave it up to him". I walked away and left her with words in her mouth. As I am walking towards the den, so I think, I really was not paying attention because Yvi really hurt my feelings. I was so focused I accidently ran right into Loard, who let out the most horrifying roar I have ever heard. It scared me, if I were not already dead, I swear I would have had a heart attack. Once I got myself together, I began to apologize, Loard I am so sorry I did not see you. I would never run into you on purpose. It is crazy everything happened so fast I blinked in the middle of my apology , out of the corner of my eye I see Mammon flying literally flying down the hallway quickly in mid-air Mammon called out a name, I really couldn't hear what he said but a bright light and a knife emerged from the air and into his hands. After that someone, I am not sure who pushed me out of the way, I tripped and landed on my but. Mammon did not hesitate, he went full force, he was going for the kill and his eyes were bright red. At this point everything was in slow motion, I seen the sword coming down at Loard and then Yvi blocked Mammon's blow with her sword. Which caught me off guard, when did she get there? Oh, she does care about someone other than herself. Just like that there was a battle between brother and sister, I quickly started to look around for Loard, I knew that blow was meant for him, but I really do not think it was intentional. I was frantic, so I called out his name. Loard? Loard where are you? Little misses I heard from behind me. I turned around and he was just staring at me. I am so sorry Loard I promise I did not see you. Little Misses no need to apologize, Little misses should never apologize to a lower demon. Huh? Loard you are not lower, and I will always apologize to my friends. Just like that Loard goes over to Mammon and Yvi who are still swinging their swords at each other, this did not look good. There was vases and Tables broken all around them, Loard go to the middle and hollered "Nostrado Extronum" He raised his hands and this green light appeared , it started to build and get bright, the minute Loard lowered his hand this loud BOOM came from the green light and both Mammon and Yvi went flying across the room.

This ends Now! He hollered. This family will stay united even if we cannot stand each other. That was an odd thing to say since their demons, but not everything is as it seems. Mammon got himself up and started dusting himself off, he started looking around for me. I quickly got up and ran to him, He hugged me and said are you okay? I thought you got hurt. No, I am fine I accidently startled Loard that is all that happened. Once I finished talking to your sister I walked out and ran into him it was a simple mistake I promise. He hugged me again this time a little harder and said I thought something happened to you. I thought the worse, I do not know what I would do if I lost you. Mammon I grabbed his face and looked at him and said Death himself cannot keep me from you and I gave him a kiss. He took a deep breath, looked at Loard and said, I am sorry my most trusted friend. What? Mammon apologized, that is new, I wonder if he is going to apologize to his sister. master, no need lets go discuss what I can here to say. Loard, Yamaries go into the Livingroom, I need to discuss something with my sister. Okay we both said and walked away, I couldn't tell you what they talked about or what the outcome was, but what I could tell you is that the talk lasted an hour and both of them came back with straight face, no expression what so ever. I cannot help being human, but curiosity killed the cat and this cat is going to die if they do not tell me something. Okay Mammon said let us begin, Loard what is it that you found? Yes master, what my informant found out is true he is keeping little misses' grandfather there and master no he does not have him in a mason jar, whatever that means. Ha, Ha I said out loud y'all are very funny, they both started to laugh I never rally heard them laugh before, it sounded a little angelic with a twist of evil. It was scary and beautiful all at the same time. Little Misses, master asked me to investigate this mason jar, why would anyone keep souls in a mason jar? Is this a human fetish? Wait, What? I started to laugh no that is not a fetish, it is where we store different non-perishable foods. Sometimes we store buttons or pins. We all began to laugh, to my surprise Yvi giggled as well. Little Misses it is going to be a great experience learning human oddities, okay all jokes to the side gentleman can someone please tell me where my grandfather is being held. He is weak Little misses Loard began, I will not lie Zozo is planning something big master and it involves the angels as well. Angels? I could not hide that I was surprise. Yes, Little misses Angels, Okay so what do we do? Now this is more than a rescue mission where on another quest to stop a war between angels and demons. Master you are king now you must decide what you want to do; remember the depiction you make it will involve all of us. I looked over at

Mammon who look stuck in deciding what to do. So, I spoke up, we are going to do this, we are going to save my grandfather's soul and stop the war. I looked over to see if Mammon would agree with me, but he did not say anything. We could do this I told him; we just must work together. My decision has been made, Loard you and I will go and save Yamaries grandfather and stop this war. Yvi you will watch Yamaries, What!? I yelled out; do not do this I am here to help not be useless. I am going with you rather you like it or not. Yamaries mammon said with authority in his voice, where we are going is dangerous there are times where I am not going to be able to help you, I will help her brother Yvi spoke out. What the F*** I am confused why is she trying to help me? You lead us through, and I will protect the rear that way we will not lose sight. Fine Yamaries if you want to come Yvi will have to come as well. That is fine with me, I said with a grin, that settles it tomorrow we begin our journey to the far deep of hell. Now let us get some rest so we could strategies in the morning. I did not know what was going to happen tomorrow, but I was prepared, so I thought. Things down here you could never prepare for.

Chapter Six

The Next morning which I thought was still night because the only light was the streetlights. There is no sundown her just darkness. Mammon got us all around the table in the kitchen to go over the plan for today. I can't believe I'm going to be saving my grandfather, if you would have asked me two years ago if I would be in hell with the prince of hell going to save my grandfather, I would look at you and baker act you. The supernatural did not exists to me, but I am glad it does. I came back to reality and I felt like I walked into a conversation mid-way, that is what I get for daydreaming. So, once we get to the man gate things are going to be crazy because by that point, he will know we will be there. So, are we ready to head out? I just smiled and said ready. Great I will just follow along mammon and Loard, I am sure they will not lead me wrong. We all walked down the hall and into a room, once you walked into the room it looked like a normal room, but mammon hit a button and the wall opened. The light came on in the hole the wall made, when I walked over to the opened wall it had stairs and it was going down in a spiral, it looks almost like a cave leading down to something. This house is a maze full of secrets, we went down the spiral stairs to arrive at a room with wall to wall weapons. I am talking about human handguns and knives. Some weapons I have never seen before. This room was every assassins dream, you think of it and it is here. Yvi looked very well in her element, me I walked over to what I knew the human guns. I do not know how to use it, but it is familiar to me and how hard could it be. Mammon Walks over to me and says, Yamaries those weapons will not work. These creatures are from the underworld that would just piss them off. Well I feel dumb, okay so what do I use? He handed me a knife at first the knife looked regular and dull like it needed to be sharpened it also have some weird writing on it. Really?! Why are you giving me this? You do not think I could handle a weapon? No, not at all Mammon said quickly, on the contrary I think you are much more powerful thank you think. This weapon thou it may look dull and useless, once someone worthy of welding it will truly shine, it is the most powerful weapon in this room. I think he is full of it, but I grabbed the sword and once it touched my I hand the sword light up. Well I guess I am full of it; see I knew you were special Mammon said with a smile. I Started to swing the sword and I almost hit Yvi. Hey girl!! She Holland at me Watch that thing! I am sorry, I… Just forget it she said. Oh okay, that was weird I was not trying to hit her on purpose, at the far end of the room there was a door locked with it is of bolts and a spell. Mammon, where does this door lead to? This door leads to wherever we are about to go but first it will lead us under the city. This place I would amazing I told myself, is everyone ready? Let us head out. When he said that all I could say in my mind was that is hot. I am such a girl, I told myself, Loard walked past me and headed towards mammon and they both raised their hand and said at the same time "Encanto Entora" and the door started to unlock. Those locks did not look ordinary and I knew they were not going to be opened with a key. The Door opened all the way and it was total darkness, I am not going to lie I did not want to go through you could not see what you were walking into. Loard Looked over at m and probably could tell that I was nervous to go through, so he said, I will go first master than little miss and yourself to follow. Misters Yvi you will follow the master and be his guard from the back. Yes, Loard I agree with that plan, Yvi did not look impressed. Loard walked through and Mammon looked at me and said you are next, I must have given an impression to Mammon that I was scared because he leaned in to me and said its okay Yamaries Loard is on the other side eating for you. I looked at him and smiled okay I told him. I worked up some nerves and walked right through of course I walked through with my hands sticking out so I make sure I would not hit anything and knock myself out. I was walking slowly shifting my feet; I could see or hear anything but my breathing and my shuffling. Out of nowhere, I seen a light and I felt a hand grab a hold of mine. I gasped a jumped back and bumped into something behind me. Little miss does not be frighten I heard, and the light got closer. Loard? Is that you? Where are you? The light got closer and Loard pops up right here little miss. I screamed and Mammon quickly covered my mouth, Shh! He said you 'd give away our position. What? Were we and who are we going to give our position to? I am sorry I whispered. I told you it was a mistake to bring her, Yvi said. I just rolled and gave her the finger; I did lol of this jester knowing that she could not see me. I do want to say I am not afraid of her, well maybe not too much of afraid of her but I do want to keep the peace mor than starting a riot. I got up slowly and Loard grabbed my hand and walked us through this portal that lead in a forest. It was weird are we back on earth? On the other hand, are we still in hell? The forest looked just like the one on earth, except for this weird moaning sound. Mammon?

What is that sound? We are in the forest of hopelessness and despair. Those are the sounds of the souls who have lost hope. My mood started to change. I started to feel sad and alone. Mammon? I do not feel so good. I told him as I started to cry, please tell me you love me. I told him. Yamaries snap out of it, your falling into their trance, you must fight it. NO! Tell me you love me! Loard! Mammon yelled out I need some assistance. Little miss if you do not fight, I am afraid of what I will do next will hurt. I could hear what Loard was trying to say but I felt I had no control. These souls kept filling sorrow and me up with their hurt. It is what Yvi said next that helped me fight my way through this. I told you brother that she is weak, she is still a mere human. Oh, hell no, she did not just say that. Okay Yamaries snap out of it, fight. I started to shake my head a little and focused so I could not hear them. I was trying to go total silent to the souls. I took deep breathers and focused on total silence. Everything started to go silent and then opened my eyes and I was begin carried in the forest. What is going on? Mammon looked at me and said you fainted, but I want to let you know you did a good job in releasing yourself from their hold. How far did we go? Where deep in the forest so we cannot go back. Just concentrate on not hearing them and you will make it through. That was easier said than done, their cry and suffering is strong, and I have a soft heart I feel it all. I tried to concentrate, and it did not take long for me to focus on saving my grandfather. I must admit I sure do know how to daydream. I did not stay focus on saving my grandfather for long the next thing I knew I started thinking about myself living in that castle, walking around in a silk red dress admiring every detail. I guess I must have been daydreaming for a while because I snapped out of it when I heard Mammon say my name. Yamaries? Umm yeah, what is wrong? Is everything okay you have been smiling and laughing for a little? Oh, ha, I smiled nothing I am okay; I finally looked around and noticed that we were coming to a cave. This cave is in the heart of the forest, it was made of logs and vines. It looks like something blow those trees down and it landed that way. We stopped right in the front of the cave. The opening looked much bigger now that I am closer. It was pitch black; you could not see anything in there. Mammon I said what are we going to use to be able to see where we are going, I mean we did not really bring a flashlight with us. Yvi started laughing typical human always-needing guidance; my brother cannot help you with everything. She really is starting to piss me off; oh, I am sorry Yvi am I bothering you with my questions. Next time I will make my question clear and directed for the intended person. Which is not you, so go fester over there somewhere, Stupid chick, I am not taking her crap no more I mumbled underneath my breath. I could be sarcastic to, bring it on sister. I looked over at mammon and said I am sorry my love, as I was saying before I was rudely interrupted. How are we going to see? He smiled and said let me show you, he raised his hand and moved it in the shape of the infinity sign and said "Xnora's Vision." His eyes changed, it was black and yellow, and they looked so beautiful. He walked over to me, touched my forehead, and said in English "Share" Just like that my vision changed. It was very bright, and I could barely see, I heard him tell me focus its hard at first, but you could alternate from day and night. It was not as easy as he makes it sound, I had a hard time because I could barely open my eyes from the light. I had my eyes closed they were burning, and I heard the sweetest voice whisper in my ear. Yamaries, calm down and relax, you are trying too hard. Listen to my voice and follow my instruction. First, my love you need to relax, I know it hurts but concentration is key.

Great how am I supposed to relax after he called me his love that, just make me more nervous. Okay Yamaries I had to tell myself, take a deep breath and get it under control. I started to take a deep breath, good Yamaries good he said. Now concentrate and just see things as normal picture it in your mind. I pictured the cave the way I seen it before I got the night vision. Are you picturing everything as normal? Yes, I have the image in my head. Good now slowly open your eyes, I was hesitant because they burned so bad, I slowly opened my eye, and everything look normal. Now when I tell you to change back into the night vision, we will do it step by step okay. Okay I said and I just stared into his eyes, he just smiled. Master shall we proceed into the cave. Yes, let proceed with caution and remember the lake is not the only thing we have to be careful about anything you see is an illusion it is all false. This cave is designed to lure you in and kill you from your hurt and despair. Oh no, something else I must try to battle, of course, I kept that to myself. We began our walk into the cave, both Loard and Yvi did the hand motion and resided the incantation, and their eyes changed. I was looking around in the cave and could barely see anything. Yamaries, it startled me when I heard his voice. I want you to concentrate and picture everything, as you would see it through night vision. I did concentrate and picture night vision. Just like that, everything was coming into view. I see things in green and black. It was perfect; the cave was amazing there was these things shining within the rocks. Mammon, what is that shining in the rocks? Those are diamonds but we have no use for them here, unlike you humans, we do not see the worth. What? He is out of his mind; these rocks are to die. Come on let us keep moving, as we are moving through the cave and getting deeper, I started to hear noise. At first, they were small, like a moan or a sigh.

Mammon did you hear that. He looked at me, Yamaries ignore it; do not pay it no mind. That was easy for him to say he is the princes of hell he has this mastered. Okay, I told him, and I tried to focus on something else. Then from behind me, I heard footsteps. I turned around and I could not see anyone there, I turned to my right and seen Yvi standing next to me. I ignored the footsteps and thought that it could have been Yvi. I kept walking and making sure I is not trip or my foot stuck in the holes. Marie was all I heard, and I jumped and looked around to see who called me. Everyone stopped and was staring at me, what? Did you all not hear that? Someone just called my name. I swear they were right by my ear. Are we going to stop every time she twitches? Brother if we keep doing this will be caught and we all will die. Yvi, calm down we are not going to die Mammon said to her. He turned to me and said Yamaries, my sister is right we will be caught and give away our position you must fight and ignore it. This is nothing compare to what is coming; every minute we waste is time we cannot get back. If he finds out where we are our adventure and chances of us saving your grandfather is gone. I am sorry to say this to you but if you end up trap or falling behind, we will continue without you, you will have to figure it out on your own. I did not respond to him because he was right, I had to keep focus because we all could end up in trap. Mammon looked at me, caressed my cheek, and said please try to keep up, Loard and Yvi lets continue. I got the feeling that he was not lying when he said he will leave me fight my own battle, I was trying so hard to look strong, but I ended up looking weak after all. I forgot where I was exactly and how different mammon is from me. I am trying so hard to be someone I am not and that is where I failed. I felt into a deep thought that I did not notice I was falling behind, Yamaries I heard that whisper again. I just kept walking and tried to ignore it. "Hey, Yamaries" and a laugh followed, the laugh stopped me in my tracks it was scary. I looked around and from behind me came the laugh again; it was like a little girl playing. "Come find me Yamaries" that is what I heard. I kept looking around as if I was lost. "Don't be afraid, I want to play." The little girl started to laugh again. I heard her laugh all around me, "Please Yamaries, let's play." "Let's play find grandpa," Ha, Ha, Ha the laugh continued. I must snap out of it, Yamaries it is all in your head. I closed my eyes and kept telling myself go away, this is not real, get it together. I finally got the voice and the laugh to stop, when I opened my eyes, I could not believe that they really left me. I could not see them anywhere. Oh no, I must hurry, I started to run and see if I could catch up. "Ha, Ha, Ha Yamaries, you are a silly girl do you really think the prince of hell could ever love?" It stopped me dead in my tracks; Leave me alone I yelled out. "Ha, Ha, Ha ya…Ma…ries who are you yelling at?" "I am not real, Ha, Ha, Ha." STOP! I yelled as I held my ears shut with my hands. I did not want to hear anything else. "Yamaries, come find me. Make me stop." Why can I still hear her? I just want her to stop. "If you come find me Yamaries I could tell you where grandpa is. Ha, ha, ha." I got up from the floor quickly and I began to run. I am not going to let this bet me. As I was running, I realized I have no idea where I was going, I just knew I had to get away from her before I lose my mind. "Ha, ha, ha Yamaries, I guess I am it, I'll catch you." I could hear her tiny footsteps running behind me. "Ha, ha, ha," she continued to laugh and giggle that was scary. I do not want to play; I am not going to play with you. "Yamaries," she wined "you hurt my feelings." Then she started to cry. "Why, why would you hurt my feelings?" "Maybe… she started to say, and she sounded Malicious. "Yes, I will… she said and trailed off again. I slowed down from running, I had to catch my breath. I leaned over and placed my hand on my knees and took a deep breath. "I… Found you" I jumped up and looked to my right. This face was right in front of me, she was pale and her eyes black, her teeth pointy with sharp edges. I screamed, she laughed and said "I…Found…You, Ha, ha, ha" I started to run through the cave, I stopped when I came to a junction. I had to pick to go through the right or left. Which way did they go? Why couldn't they just wait? Or at least leave me a sign. "Ha, ha, ha what is the matter Yamaries? Can't find your way?" "In order to continue you have to choose, this is one of my favorite games." "So, which is it Yamaries, right or left?" I cannot think when you are talking to me. I do not know which one to choose. I have made plenty of difficult decisions in my life, but I could not make this easy decision. "Come on Yamaries." Her voice went from a sweet little girl to a snarling demon like voice. "Choose, your destiny awaits you." Please STOP! Leave me alone. "I'll give a little hint, one of these opening will lead you down the path to your true love, Mammon. The Other, well we will just say you belong to us." "Ha, ha, ha its laugh was so scary and high pitched. That it just made everything worse. "Choose Yamaries! Choose!" I could not flip a coin so I did the next best thing, I it Eeny Meany Miny Moe, I know it is not practical, but it is the best I could think about under pressure. So, I looked at the two opening and began, to my surprise my finger was pointing to the opening on the right. "Go on walk through it" "Ha, ha, ha" I couldn't go through with it, I am not sure what was guiding me towards the left ,but that is exactly where I went, I started to run towards the opening on the left hoping in my heart that it would lead me the right way. Once I went through the pitch-black opening, I got dizzy. I closed my eyes and once I reopened my eyes Loard, Mammon and Yvi where staring at me. "Yamaries, are you okay?

Mammon asked. Huh? When did I catch up to you? I was so confused I swear I was way behind them. What is she talking about? Yvi asked Mammon she did not look amused at all, she almost looked at me as if I was lying. I was a little bit upset about her remark so I said you guys left me, you said if I can't catch up you would leave me behind, and I would have to find my way. Yamaries, we have been standing here for fifteen minutes no one has said that we were going to leave you. Mammon looked so confused in what I was saying. Brother, she was trapped, they brought her to their side. I am glad you were able to let yourself out, I am glad to know that you could do stuff on your own. Was she trying to be funny or is she being an a-hole? forget that its Yvi of course she is being a smart ass. That Bitch, I thought to myself. I could not keep my cool, I just lost it I am sorry Yvi did I do something to upset you so much that your being rude. I can't take your shit anymore, I might not have a lot of training in fighting but please do not let this little frame fool you, I am from Chi-town I know how to scrap. She had this very confused look on her face. Brother what is she talking about? You have been around humans long enough. Nothing sister let us keep moving he replied to her. NO! I yelled she is going to answer my question, why are you so mean to me? I have not done anything to you. Right now, I do not that you have my back. Yamaries right now is not the time, we are in the middle of this cave with many obstacles, we need to press on. Yvi looked surprised that I would say anything. I got closer to her so she could hear me clearly, this is not over, I told her and walked away. I was enraged how can he just stop me in the middle of my argument. I walked past Mammon and stood right next to Loard. We were walking, a couple of feet in front of mammon and Yvi, I needed some space. I was in my own thoughts when Loard spoke, Little Miss? Huh, yes Loard?

Good work on standing up for yourself. He made me smile, thank you Loard. Ms. Yvi is not always this mean, believe it or not she did smile once. A long, long, long time ago. We both laughed, Ms. Yvi is just jealous of your love for the master, she could tell it is true love. She fears she will never have that for herself. Well that still does not give her the right, I could not even finish that sentence I felt so bad. Why do I have to be so nice? She will find it one day, maybe if she stops her ugly attitude she might get somewhere. Ms. Yvi is a fierce warrior that is all she knows and trying to have demons down here to respect her, we will let us just say once you get that it is hard to go back. I guess I understand, just as if I knew you would little miss, you know you are different from other humans. I am not sure what it is, but it is nice. I smiled at him and said see Loard I knew you would warm up to me. I know this is mean but Loard smiled and that was the scariest thing I have ever seen. I think I might have twitched a little. Where almost at the river of soul, little miss. When we get on the boat, do not little miss and I do mean DO NOT look at the boat keeper. Great, now I am going to have to look. Okay but Loard why? Did I just really ask why, I have a feeling I am not going to like the answer. Little Miss I am going to tell you because, little miss you are a very curious one so I know you will look. I this said that the boat keeper has no face but staring into the dark space where his face should be you will fall into a pit of darkness. A space of nothingness, of course little miss this is a rumor no one who has really seen his face ever came back to speak of it. Well look at that little miss, I starting to think like a human, he smiled again. Oh man, I wish he would stop smiling, it is creeping me out. Right Loard, I will do my best not to look. I do not want to find out if that rumor is true. Oh, and little miss try not to look at the river either, I have grown fawned of you. Okay Loard, I said with a smile, little miss I am not joking I have seen what happens to spirits who cannot help themselves and looked. It will hurt me to see that happen to you, but it will destroy my master. We demons live-forever a pain of loss is a pain everlasting. I understand Loard, I know you are also trying to protect mammon. I will do my best, how close are we? We will be there shortly; look ahead do you see that bright light? Yes, I do, I said with excitement, that is where we are headed. Loard leaned into said little miss and I go ahead and change from night vision; you are going to want to see this. I went ahead and got my vision back to normal and I have to say Loard was right the view of this cave was breath taking, for it to be so dangerous. I could see why people could just get hypnotized. The Beautiful blue and green hitting the black cave was amazing. The blue of the diamonds on the cave floor looks like I was walking through a field of majestic flowers. The green was coming from the river, which was carrying, the souls. I was so memorized and confused all at the same time, I just could not rap my head around this place being so dangerous. Loard and I got to the river first, I did not notice that we walked ahead, so Loard and I were at the river quite for a little, it was somewhat awkward. I was going to ask Loard a question, but I see Mammon and Yvi from the corner of my eye, it looks like they were in deep conversation. I hope they were not talking about a strategy. Mammon looked over my way, I locked eyes with him, and my heart melted. I cannot be mad at him it was not his fault after all. He just did not want a confrontation between his sister and me, there was something different in his eyes, and he looks somewhat upset. I turned to Loard, he was looking across the river, and there it was the boat. It was gliding across, almost as if it were floating. The boat was all black, at first it looks like a regular boat but as it started getting closer the boat look like it had a hand sticking out of it. I was watching the boat so closely I never noticed that Mammon was standing right next to me. Yamaries stay close Mammon said seriously. He startled me; I looked over at him and said okay. I looked back at the boat and my suspicion was right, this boat was made of human bones. Is that boat really made of bones? I said aloud. Yes, Mammon answered quickly. These were sacrificed human remains. In other word they are tortured humans, my eyes got wide, I said, and we are getting in that? Yes, Mammon answered this is our only transportation. Mammon I thought we were not supposed to tell anyone about our arrival. Well he said the thing driving the boat is very trustworthy. It does not have a face of its own; also, no one really looks at it… yes, I interrupted I know Loard told me already; I will not take that chance and look at it. Ha, Ha, Ha he started to laugh, what is so funny? Loard can over exaggerated, He was just having some fun. The boat driver is okay to look at nothing will happen; he is just a strong silent type as you human would put it. Huh? Wait, all of that was a lie? Mammon looked at me and smiled and said yes, we tell this to the little demons so they could listen and not venture off. Okay that is the craziest thing to tell little… I trailed off then I realized where I was wait, okay I get it. Whatever, I rolled my eyes. The boat was stopped and this ramp cane down, even the ramp was made from bones, it was nasty to walk on. I could hear the ones crunching and snapping as I walked on it. Once I got on, I seen a hoodies thing holding the wheel that navigates the boat. I could not help it and looked at its face. I was taken aback when I realized there was nothing there, but a black whole of nothingness. How is he navigating? The hands holding the wheel was a skeleton and it had no feet. The thing was very tall, it towered over the boat. That was scary, you were not supposed to look at its little miss remember.

Ha, Ha Loard very funny, I hope you had a good laugh because you will not get me again. I smiled at him; it shall be fun trying little miss he said with a smile. The boat started to move again at first it was smooth but then it started to get a little rocky, unfortunately my spirit still thinks I am in a body because I got seasick. I quickly ran to the side of the boat so I could throw up, well so I thought. Mammon yelled Yamaries do not! But it was too late I was already leaning over the railing and I opened my eyes. There they were souls hundreds of thousands of souls. At first, they did not notice me, they were white and looked so lost. I could not stop staring and I had this overwhelming feeling of needing to help them. To set them free as if they were hurting, I guess I didn't notice but a piece of chipped bone was dangling and I moved my hand accidentally hit it and in slow motion I seen the piece of bone hit the river. Oh no, I said and just like that as if they were all united, they looked up at me. That was all it took. I was trapped, now I had to get myself out of this a mess. I slowly feel into a trance looking deep into their eyes and passing through space and into their souls. I felt a little dizzy I blinked and just like that I was in Mammon's room in the house where he made up when he was in me. I looked around and everything looked the same. How did I get here? I looked down and noticed that I was in a red gown. The gown was beautiful, it was long silky material with a mesh top with sparkling glitter, the dress was elegant. It felt a little odd but nevertheless I felt at home. I also notice the fireplace was on, I started to look around the room and touch the bed post and to all felt real. Did the boat drive take me back here? I walked over to the door grabbed the doorknob and I froze. I was afraid to open the door, instead I placed my ear against the door to listen and see if anyone was on the other side. I heard a little movement it sounded as if it was walking back and forth in front of my door. What was it? Is it Mammon? Suddenly, the walking stopped, Huh? I wonder where it went. I tried to concentrate to see if I could hear something more, I even slow down my breathing. Just like that a loud pounding came from the door, I jumped and fell backwards landing on my butt. What the hell was that? Then three more pounds came from the door, it was so hard I thought the door was going to fly open. I was frozen in that spot; I was so scared to move. Then a bad smell was coming from underneath the door, it was a smell of rotten flesh. The smell was so bad I thought I was going to vomit, I snapped myself out of it and started to stand up. The pounding began again this time it did not stop. It kept pounding over and over again, I ran to the double doors that usually would end up on the balcony looking over the waterfall and the trees, but when I opened the door it was complete darkness. There was no escape, where am I? I wanted to cry from the overwhelming feeling of the door pounding and not knowing. LEAVE ME ALONE! I yelled. The pounding stopped and this laugh that I remember all so well came from behind the door. Ya...Ma...ries have you missed me? He, He. I have missed you, come on let us play. Mammon is her too, Mammon? I said he is there with you? Yes, he is standing right next to me, come open the door so you could see for yourself. Let us in Yamaries, NO! I do not believe you. I need to hear his voice, Now Yamaries would I ever lie to you? Yamaries, it was him, that was his voice. Yamaries are you in there? Open the door let me in, I felt my heart skip a beat. My fears were gone I felt safe, h was here with me. Mammon hold on I am going to open the door. I thought I was alone here; I quickly ran to the door and was going to open it but then he said. Yamaries my beloved opens the door, I cannot wait to hold you in my arms, I need to hold you forever. I stopped dead in my track, that was not mammon he would never say that. No, you are not mammon, who are you? Well, Well I guess there is no living to you dear Yamaries. Open the door Yamaries lets play. You will be happy here with us, we are always playing here. No this is not real. I finally realized what was going on. I am caught in the river of souls; I must snap out of it. This is not real I kept saying, I closed my eyes. Please Yamaries snap out of it, I felt dizzy and I opened my eyes and all I could see was the souls in the river closer to me, the water was touching the tip of my nose. Mammon! I yelled, Yamaries, we got you, he said quickly. Slowly I was being pulled up, little miss is you okay? Yes, just I please pull me up. I was finally on the boat and quickly hugged Loard and Mammon. Thank you for saving me, I thought I would never get out of that place. Yamaries, I think you might be the first person to be able to fight your way out of the river of souls. Little miss, master is right how did you do it? There was something the little girl demon said while she was pretending to be mammon, that I knew in my heart he would not say or talk in that way. Mammon smiled, I knew you would get out of it, you are a fighter. I felt a little sick again, so I sat down and closed my eyes for a little, Little Miss? Loard said Yamaries? Mammon said I guess I did not answer Loard fast enough, are you okay? They both said it at the same time. Yes, guys I am fine, I am just a little dizzy. I need a little time and I will be back and ready to face whatever is next, the guys moved away a little not too far it was like they were cautions. Yvi surprisingly walked over to me, Yamaries? Yvi I am not going to argue with you right now. Who said I was coming over here to argue? I was checking on you, so my brother could see I am trying to be nice, but if you want to argue we can. As a matter of fact, I will walk away, forget I even came over. No, I manage to open my eyes, thank you for checking on me. I am sorry for being so snappy I am not feeling so well. Who knew that I would have motion sickness? She looked at me and said it is from coming back, just give it sometime and it shall pass. You fought your way out of two places, a soul could not be able to get out of one let alone two. You are stronger than you look, I have never encounter someone like you. You may not have much combat skills, but you have a lot of heart and well that is not something you see every day. You have erranded my respect, she started to walk away, she stopped mid-way and said keep making him happy. I have her eye contact and she half smiled and kept walking. Wow, did she just warm up to me. I lowered my head and closed my eyes and smiled to myself. I must have fallen asleep which I did not know U still could do, but I was awoken by Mammon, Yamaries? Are you okay? Wha... I said slowly huh. I am sorry I must have dosed off. That is okay, you have been through so much you deserve some rest. We are arriving close to the first gate of the underworld. Once we arrive, rest will be no more. The places through each gate is different and extremely hard to get through, we all must stick together and as you say have each other's back. Umm? Each gate? Yes, he said there is eight gates, each is built with a different dimension that will test all your ability. I am out to worried about you; you will do great. He smiled at me and said, you know I love the fact that you always seem to surprise me this is why I was so intrigued with you in the beginning and why I am so in love with you now. For the first time in a while I was speechless, I could feel the heat rising on my face. I am sure my face was flushed; I love you to was all I could mustered up to say. I mean what can you say after that, he kept smiling and said come we are arriving let me show you the entrance of the first gate. We both got up and walked over to the side of the boat. What I seen was insane how could something that is breath taking be a part of the eight gates of hell. The gate was huge, it looked like it went up a long way. It was bright gold, very shiny. The gate was Venice style dual entry, if you did not know better you would think that you were going towards the gates of heaven. Wait? Are they mocking the pearling gates of heaven? Goodness no, well, it is fitting to lower souls in to thinking they are reaching heaven, that is a sick joke. We were starting to get close to the gate and I was wondering how we are going to dock. As the thought was going. Through my head the boat started to collect some fog around it. This is odd, then the boat began to change, it started to get smaller. I felt someone touch my shoulder, at first, I thought it was Mammon but when I looked it was the hooded boat drier. It scared me; it did not speak but pointed at the middle of the boat. I slowly walked over to the middle with Loard and Yvi. Mammon was still looking out the side of the boat, the hooded boat driver walked over to him, they looked like they were having a conversation. Mammon bowed his head in agreement and started to walk towards us, in that instance the bones of the boat stated to come off and come together. What the hell? The bones where starting to make skeletons. It was about ten of them. They were standing in attention, they hooded boat driver pointed outside of the boat and the skeleton's jumped into the water. The Boat came to a complete stop and the anchor feel as it did it screamed a deadly scream and a platform was built of bones came out and hit the ground. We walked past the hooded boat driver and I swear it said be safe. Just like that we were faced to face with the golden gate.

Chapter Seven

There we were facing this big gate and the only thing I was thinking about was how are we going to get in. Is there a password, do we knock? I hope no one must sing, we will never get in. Loard and Yvi pushed back a little and mammon walked closer to the gate. I walked over to Loard and Yvi, I turned to them and said what she going to do? Little miss the master is going to do an old incantation. He is now the king of hell and can-do special incantations. Oh, okay well that sounds easy enough. Loard, Yvi said tell her everything, my brother has never done anything like that before, the hooded boat driver so you call him. Gave my brother the incantation, I am not even sure if my father ever done it. Okay, I believe he can do it, he is not y'all's dad, I think he will be better. Yvi rolled her eyes, no you are not understanding she said, I heard Mammon start the incantation "Dominos Lumos Enferno." What am I not understanding Yvi? "Inferno Dana's exteriors" Yamaries! She yelled he could die. These gates are not supposed to be forced open. They only open to a soul who us in desperate need. "Enos Fantasma Unos" Mammon kept on going. I do not know why but I was frozen, I did not move at all. I think my mind was not firing fast enough for my body to respond. Yvi looked at me with her eyes wide as if telling me to stop him, but I could not move fast enough. I finally got myself to turn towards Mammon, I could hear Yvi say hurry he is going to say the last verse of the incantation. I am not sure why this happens but whenever I try to do something quickly, I go slower. It is a mystery to me, I started to try and run towards Mammon and I could hear him start the last verse. "Serfona eous…" I finally reached him and through my body on top of his and yelled NO! please do not Mammon! I started to cry and just held him my heart hurt so much from thinking that I was going to have to live without him. As I was crying and holding him, I heard some cling noise. I looked at Mammon, who eyes had a stunned look on his face. I looked over at the gate and to my surprise the gate starts to open. Umm, was that supposed to happen? I asked mammon, h did not answer he just looked surprised. I did not notice when Yvi and Loard got to us but Loard quickly answered my question. No, little miss that should have never happened.

We were all staring at the gate, while it was open. Should we go through it or are we going to just stare at it? We are being precautions; we do not understand how that gate opened. Did Mammon say the last verse? Yvi asked, I am not sure I told her. I know he was in the middle of the last verse, but I am not sure if he said the last word before I got there. I think Yamaries opened the gate, Mammon said after a long time of silence. Huh? How? I said in confusion. Yvi answered with a soul in desperate need. This heifer just called me desperate, Yvi what do you mean? You did not want to lose Mammon, so you through yourself on him in desperation. To lose me. Mammon said like if he was thinking it over in his head. Yvi what are you talking about? I had a dumb look on my face, excuse me did you not tell me if Mammon says the last verse he could die. Mammon how could you not tell me that you could have died if you say these verses, we could have done something else or find another way in. Yamaries what are you talking about Mammon said, the verse could have never killed me I am immortal I can't die one and two it is just words all it could do is make me extremely tired. I started to get angry, I turned to Yvi How could you lie to me like that! That scared me half to death if I were not already dead it would have. Oh, Yamaries do not be so dramatic, you cannot die twice but now I know for sure that your heart is true to my brother. WHAT?! Yamaries please do not yell they will hear us. Mammon if you tell me to be quite one more time you and I will have a problem. Just as I finished the sentence the gates started to close. We must move Mammon said, I looked at Yvi and said Bitch, I am coming for you. I took off running towards the gate. Yamaries wait mammon yelled out. I cannot I yelled back the gate is closing. I ran right through, Loard and mammon where right behind me. Little miss you should not run through like that; you do to know what is on the other side. Loard I really do not care what is on the other side because being next to Yvi is the hardest battle than anything I will have to face, being around her is torment everything else is a cake walk. I started to walk away, and Mammon ran after me, Yamaries? Mammon said I really do not care what you have to say right now. I am not sure my sister came through. Mammon I frankly do to give a crap, she could stay out there and wait for all I care. I was sort of lying in a sense I did not want her to die out there without us, so I looked around and seen Loard was with her. See your precious sister is being accompanied by Loard she is fine. Can we push on now? No, we need to stay together remember. Oh, please keep hr ass over there. I started walking off, I did not know how much of this I could take. Her lies and his intent to protect his little sister. She could be an asshole, but I cannot help it. I told myself. I kept walking going deeper and deeper in, I never noticed what my surroundings look like. I felt someone grabbed my hand almost as if they wanted me to stop. Mammon please I just need to… When I turned to look no one was there. That is when I snapped back and started to look around. I noticed that everything looked like the woods behind my grandmother's house. Wait, What? Where am I? Am I home? I keep looking around and noticed the trees and the grass and an incredibly special plant that I planted a year ago in memory of my grandfather. I started to cry, I missed him so much. I started to walk over to the plant. I am home, this cannot be fake because they would have never known about the flower. I sat in front of the flower and just cried. I failed all I wanted to do was save you grandpa, I do not want you to be aloe. I was deep in my hurt and someone placed their hand on my shoulder. I looked up and no one was there. I wiped my tears away and thought to myself, that is odd I am sure someone touched me. I turned back around to look at the flower and I was gone. Wait, where did it go? I took another glance around and everything was gone. All I could see was rocks and thin heat and steam. Mammon? I yelled out. Mammon where are you? Why did not I just listen, I get so hardheaded. Now I have lost him, I got up from the floor and I looked around I could not see anyone. Yamaries is not this what you wanted? It was a man's voice a creepy, cranky man voice. This is exactly what you wanted, to be alone. No! I never wanted that, yes you did in fact you desired it so strongly, I could not help but grant you that. No, I never said that. Oh Yamaries, He, he laughed you do not need to say anything here your heart does the talking. No, then you know that this is not what I want. Well you are right, because you figured it out so quickly, I will give you him back.

Yamaries? Mammon is that you/ I replied to someone calling for me. I see him walking towards me and I ran to him and held him. Are you okay? Yes, I am so sorry I should not have walked away. Well, well if it is not the one and only Prince of hell. What do you want with her? Mammon stated as a matter of fact. Now, Now Prince you might be a big shot in hell but here you are nothing. Stay close he is very tricky and quick, Mammon whispered to me. Now, Little miss Yamaries lets play a game shall we, we turned over and seen Loard and Ivy they were tied up and being beaten. No! Stop Please! I yelled I could see the blood just flying from their mouth and hitting the floor but why. Is not this what you wanted? He asked. No, this is never what I wanted. I could feel that you do, but not for this one, so Loard dropped to the ground. I ran to Loard and hugged him; I tried to clean him up. I am so sorry Loard I wanted you hurt. Whoever you are you will pay for hurting him. Whoever I am well let me introduce myself and out he came out from the shadows I am Jairo and I am the keeper of the gate of desires, he was normal looking. Average height, pale with green eyes, he was wearing a tuxedo with a top hat and had a cane. This through me for a loop, I was expecting ugly and gruesome. I got up from where I was at and started to walk towards him. Mammon grabbed me and said do not be a fool; he is much stronger than you think. Jairo, what do you want from me? Well I thought I told you that already. You are not a particularly good listener; I want to play a game. Mammon, said what kind of game? No, Prince the game is snot with you Jairo said with a smile, I have no use for you here in my realm. I just need your sweet human Yamaries, it is amazingly simple, and it will not take long at all. If you win what happens? I asked quickly since it looks like he is only going to answer to my request. Oh, he giggled this is getting interesting, so you agree to play the game. Yamaries, I do not think this is a good idea, Mammon sounded a little concerned and that is not like him, so I started to get a little nervous. What else are we supposed to do; I do not think he will let us continue without playing. Well, Yamaries? I do not like repeating myself, so time is up play or not. His voice got scary and angry; well I guess I have no choice let us play. GREAT! He sounds overly excited, let us begin. All you must do is answer one question and Yamaries you must tell the truth; I will know if you are lying. Okay, Jairo so what do I get if I win? Yes, yes you human souls are all the same. If you win, I will transport you straight to gate number two personally, and if I lose? I told him you belong to me. He said that Very creepy, No! Mammon yelled you would never have her. Jairo looked at Mammon and his green eyes changed to bright red; Prince do not test me! He growled. Okay, I agree I said, and I started to tear up. No, Yamaries do not, I am not afraid let us play. I said that with a lot of confidence, but I really was scared. He, he, he yes let us play, he waved his cane, and everything changed. We were standing in my grandparent's living room sort of, half of the living room had the couches and stairs and the other half looked like a dungeon. There was Yvi in a cage beaten, cuts and bloody. My heart hurt, I felt so bad. Now sweet Yamaries come get comfortable I want you to be relax as you can. Jairo you are delaying time, time I do not have so let us get to it. You will do well not to piss me off! He yelled. Now come and sit! I quickly walked over to the couch and sat down. Comfortable? He asked nicely. This Demon is nuts I said to myself, yes thank you I am okay. Good now my question to you is... He just stopped and smiled. I just stared at him and did not say anything

I was afraid that he would lose it. NO, NO this is all wrong your heart changed, but your desire is still the same. Let us make this interesting, he snapped his finger and up came Mammon in a cage as well. NO! STOP! This was not part of the game. Neither was your heart but we all cannot help how we feel. Please, please do not hurt him, I begged him. Why Sweet Yamaries that is all up to you, as he said that with a smile. He began to turn his cane and two little ugly monsters jump out from the ground. They were horrifying, they bended and twisted like if someone pulled them apart and put them back in the wrong way like a sick joke. They were slimy and drolly, their teeth were sticking out. Come here my boys, where are my boys? He was calling them over like dogs. Yes, daddy loves you, now boys listen go by the cage and await my commands. I have a feeling you are going to have fun today. I was starting to get a little nervous and uneasy. How am I going to get out of this? I started to look around maybe try to find a way out of this or something, anything I was getting desperate. I did notice that Loard was not here, I see Yvi and Mammon but not Loard. Where he has placed him, I said to myself. Now Yamaries I am ready to play. I am feeling that today might be my lucky day; I rolled my eyes, I Felt like the one, he was stalling. There was something up his sleeves, he is a liar and very sneaky. Yamaries my question and once again please answer truthfully, what are your true desires? Okay, huh? I was so confused with that question. This is going to be a little more complicated than I thought. I looked over at him and he was just standing there smiling. I wanted to wipe that smile off; it is funny how human spirts have found this question to be the hardest. Search deep you will find your answer, but remember their lives, Prince and Princess aside they can die. So Yamaries have you found your answer, I have all eternity but you I have this strong sensation that you are in a rush. What I desire… I trailed off, and then I started to cry, I just want my parents back. I lost it, I mean full blown, chest hurting with boogers and all. I am not sure why, but I did, it felt good. Well, well sweet little Yamaries, you are the first human soul to tell the truth. I am impressed and bored, please stop your crying it is annoying. Just because I am true to my word, I will take you to the second gate. Okay, I said and wiped my face. He raised his cane and waved it in the shape of a circle and a portal apparated. Inside the portal I could see the second gate, hurry up I do not have all day he said. Huh? You need to let them go. Oh no, no my sweet Yamaries I never said anything about letting them go. I said I will take you to the second gate personally. NO! that was not the deal and you know it. Next time be more specific when you want something, every detail counts down here in the deepest parts of hell. Believe me, I will not be the only one making you suffer. Please do not do this we had a deal, I cried out to him. Humans are so disgusting crying for everything, loving everyone, hurting each other, you are all the same, sweet Yamaries nothing in this part of hell is fair. Now go through the portal! He growled. No not without them, them? Now sweet Yamaries are you lying to me? Do you mean, him? You do not care about her, as a matter of fact why do not, we let the sweet prince know exactly how you feel about the princess. This is going to be fun, go on tell him. He waved his hand and a chair came up from the ground and he sat on it. He was enjoying this way too much. I had to think quick, oh and sweet Yamaries do not lie, I hate liars. Bingo, his demand now it is my turn, okay I will not lie but in return you must let everyone go, that includes Loard, Mammon and Yvi…. He cut me off before I could finish. Oh, is that so, well, well looks like you are my type of girl, you pick up very quickly. Is that all? No and you must make a portal and send us all through it to the second gate. You are a little demanding, little miss Yamaries, he smiled, I like that okay I will grant you that. So, tell us Yamaries, tell us how you really feel, I love human stories. His smile was just as demonic as his tone. I should have thought this through a little better, I am not sure now Mammon is going to react. Okay here hoes. Jairo, I do not care much for his sister Yvi, I do not care if she keeps on with us on this Journey. Quite frankly I want to beat the crap out of her. She has this I am better than everyone complex and she is very unfriendly. She really needs to get out more and socialize. Once I began, I could not stop. I was waiting to say all that stuff and Finally got to. Well, well Yamaries this is something I love, now tell us how you really feel, he said sarcastically. Despite all that Jairo if you must know, I would never, ever let someone else hurt her that is my job. He, he, he that is it, I was hoping one day I would meet someone like you. Okay, here you go he waved his hands, and both fell out of their cages. He smiled and pointed with his wand and Loard appeared. I ran over to Mammon, Loard and Yvi. Once I got to Mammon, I tried to hold him, but he pushed me away. Oh no, I had a feeling he was going to be mad at me. I looked at him and noticed he was still tied up. Huh? Wait? I looked over at Yvi and Loard was trying to untie her as well. What is this? You were supposed to let them free. No, you said let them go and I did. Now here is your portal to the second gate. They cannot move how are they going to get through the portal? That my Sweet is not my concern. I have done my part the rest is up to you. Oh, and before I forget the portal will close in approximately twenty minutes and counting. HA! HA! Good luck, he snapped his fingers and he was gone. That tricky little… ahh!! I yelled. Loard we do not have much choice we are going to have to get them through the portal ourselves. I could lift the little miss but how are we going to get the master through. Start heading to the portal I got him go now, Loard bowed his head and lifted Yvi and ran. I started to look around franticly to see if I could think or find something.

Lady luck was on my side, Jairo left the table with the torture tools on it, I quickly got up and ran to the table. I knocked everything off the table as fast as I could and started rolling it towards mammon, out of the corner of my eye I seen something it was moving quickly. I ignored it and quickly got to mammon, now how am I going to get him up there? Then again something moved, what is that? I started to look around, but mammon began to speak. We need to hurry; the portal is about to close, and I think we have visitors. Right but I need your help, can you move a little? Yes, he answered. Good let get you on this table and we can roll out of here. I helped him up and placed him on the table once he was on the table, I heard footsteps and giggling coming from behind me. I looked at Mammon and said what is behind me? His eyes where wide and he said RUN! We got to run. I began pushing the cart towards the portal, which looks like it was about to close. Does that portal look a smaller than before? I asked Mammon. Yamaries we need to hurry. I know, do not get like that it makes me nervous. The portal started to get smaller right in front of my eyes, oh crap I tried to get there faster the portal gets further away. Wait this is his doing, I will kill that guy, mammon I am getting tired. I am not sure if we are going to make it. Yes, we are do not think like that, I knew exactly what was going on and what I must do. I looked at mammon and said I love you, but this must be done. Find my grandfather and set him free, I pushed the cart with all my might and watched it get to the portal. I knew this is exactly what Jairo wanted. I could not hear Mammon, but I could see what he was mouthing out. Do not do this, everything went in slow motion, I felt like the whole world was coming down on me. The cart and Mammon went through the portal and I just stared. I began to cry because I knew this was going to be my reality. Now why did you do that? Jairo said, where are you? I asked him. You are a lying piece of crap. All I ever wanted was a friend, it gets lonely down here Yamaries. Then you had to go do something so noble. Self-Sacrifice, that bores me, Jairo sounded frustrated I will let you go through I am bored with you. Now go, I will let the god of the second gate have some fun with you. Now that demon is no Jairo his is all business and no fun, go now leave my home, just like that Jairo waved his cane and some force pushed me so hard I flew right into the portal and landed right on Loard. I did not mean to… He quickly cut me off and said little miss it was not your fault. As the portal started to close you could hear Jairo's laugh that creepy laugh. What a piece of crap, I said to myself. I looked over at Mammon who looked like someone ran all over is emotions. Yvi was next to him comforting him, I looked at Loard and said do you think I should give them a minute? They look like their having a moment. No, no little miss you need to go hold the master he thinks he has lost you. I started to get up and I noticed that they did not have restraints anymore. Loard, how did they get the restraints off? Once they got through the portal little miss is like they never had them. Well that is weird, I am only glad they do not have them anymore. I was going to take a step, but I turned to Loard and said do you think Yvi and Mammon are upset at me for what I said? Hard to say little miss a lot has just happened, just go, and let the master see you, then we will deal with the rest. Okay, I was still a little hesitant, but I started walking over to Yvi and Mammon, I was not expecting the results that happened, both mammon and Yvi gave me a hug. That is right Yvi hugged me, shocked me too. I never thought I would see you again Mammon said. Yvi looked at me and smiled and walked towards Loard. You Cannot get rid of me that easy I told him; I never want to get rid of you. Hey, I am sorry for everything I said about your sister, it was not something I wanted to share. That does not matter, what matters is that you sacrificed yourself to only to save your grandfather but us as well. No one, not even our father would have done that for us. You all are my family that is how I feel, and we are a team, we do better together not separate. Besides, I knew you, Yvi and Loard would have made it and saved my grandfather. You never stop amazing me, Mammon said and smiled. Now let see how where going to get into that gate, I smiled at him and looked over at that gate, but it was not a gate it was more of a door, okay, that is different. Loard and Yvi came closer and said you are right is not it supposed to be a gate. I decided to walk closer to the door, and it reminded me of a cottage door. Wait! Yvi said I am not sure… I got to the door and I was reaching for the doorknob to see if it would open, but there were these strange noises coming from behind the door. I think my body and mind where not communicating because I decided that it was smart for me to place my ear against the door. I placed my right hand against the door right next to my ear as if that would make the noise any louder, but what I did next was so dumb and I did it without thinking, I took my left hand and grabbed hold of the doorknob and just like that I was inside of a room. I looked around and it was dark, very dark and I felt lonely. Mammon? I said are you there? I cannot see anyone. Yvi, Loard, are you there? Hello… came a hissing voice. So, you are the Yamaries that Jairo told me about, how remarkably interesting. What do you want? You do go straight to business, even though I could not see anything I did try to look around and find something. Where is Mammon, Yvi and Loard? Do not worry so much, they are not in here with you. The Prince and Princess cannot come in. They are not welcome here; I was going to ask about Loard, but he cut me off before I could begin. The servant I just do not like him, Lucifer's little pet. Do not talk about him in that way I snapped. My, my what a temper he said I love that. I do not like that you care so much, that is ugly of you. All we want to do is go through and get to the third gate. Such in a hurry, stay, sit lets chat. I do not have time; we need to keep going with all these introductions just tell me what I must do to get to the third gate. SSS... ha, ha ... you think I like to play games... SSS, ha, ha I AM NOT JAIRO!! He roared and the room began to shake. Jairo has the mind of a child; I am not sure how he became a gate keeper. Now sit and relax, this will not take too long. Where exactly am I going to sit? There is nothing... and just like that there was a table and two chairs. Please sit, he said slowly go ahead I will not SSS bite. I really doubt that I told myself. I walked over to the chair and sat down. Now Yamaries let us chat. How can I chat with you when I cannot even see you, that is rude? Oh, my where are my manners SSS.... I looked around to see where he would be coming from but instead of a person, I seen a pair of green eyes with a black slit in the middle. I tried to see if it had a body, but It did not it was just a black smoke cloud shaped as a body. I could see it getting closer to the other chair. It was creepy and all I could do was stare. I tried to stop looking at its eyes, but I was stuck just staring. I started to feel a little lightheaded and this over whelming feeling of loneliness. Now Yamaries lets begin, tell me how did you feel when your mother died? What? Wait, why? Just look at my eyes Yamaries, concentrate and tell me how you felt when your mother died. I feel into a trans and I began to speak, it was as if I was in a fog. I was in a lot of pain; I lost my best friend and the person that believed in everything I did. Where you alone? No, I had my dad. No, Yamaries look at me. I looked at it again and I got deeper and deeper into the trans.

Tell me Yamaries did you feel lonely? Yes, I said at first, but then I had to be strong for my dad. SSS.... This will not do, let us go deeper, Yamaries tell me how did you feel to lose your dad? It hurt; I lost the only parent I had left... I started to try and fight the trans, but it was hard. Oh, SSS... you are a fighter. Then I see this black smoke coming towards me I tried to move, but I could not. The smoke touched my forehead and strange enough it was cold. Once it touched me, I went back in my memory and straight into the day I got the knock on the door, when I found out my dad died. Oh no, I must relive this day, there was a knock on the door, I blinked, and it was as if I was there again. I sat up on the couch and looked around. I am back at my old house, I heard another knock and my heart skipped a beat, I could hear my aunt saying I am coming. I laid right back on the couch and told myself this is not happening, I do not want to, please do not do this. Feel it Yamaries feel the pain of loneliness. Hi, how may I help you? My aunt was saying, I knew it was the two cops. OH NO! I got up quickly and ran to the door, instead of standing in front of the door I stood behind the door. Yamaries? I heard my aunt say. Please aunty do not tell me. I am so sorry, everything started going in slow motion. NO! I said this will not hurt me, it was a long time ago I have people that love me, and I do not feel lonely at all. Just like that I was on the chair again. Well, well I am impressed, you got yourself out of that. Well Okay if you insist, I guess since you do not have any more stories of loneliness, I will let you go. It waved its smokey hand and the cottage door appeared. Go on go through and you will be at gate number three. Will they be there? yes, all three will be there he said with this monotone voice. Why are you telling me to go? I just got out of your trans. Yes, you did, and it bores me, your stories no longer hurt as much. I got up from the chair and walked over to the door, I looked over at it and he said safe travels. I swear I could hear it smiling. I opened the door and walked through, sure enough they were there, I ran up to them and just hugged them all. I am glad you guys are okay, what happened? Yvi asked. There was this thing and it was trying to make me feel… I stopped myself and said never mind, just know that I got out of it and we are here. Okay, but where is here? Yvi said. Nice it lied; I am not sure he was supposed to place us right at gate number three, but I should not be surprised. Okay let us fine this third gat Mammon said, Lets go this way. We all stared to walk through this dark cave I changed my eye quickly to night vision and noticed that Yvi and Mammon where discussing something, Huh, I wonder what that is about. I was walking over to Mammon and Yvi when someone grabbed my arm. I got startled and looked to see who grabbed me, oh Loard its you, I am sorry I am a little jumpy lately. You should be a little miss you have been through a lot in just a short period of time. Little miss, please do not interrupt their conversation. What are you talking about I was going to ask them if they are discussing a plan because I want in. Little miss if they wanted to tell you they would leave them be. What? Loard what are you talking about? We should be included now excuse me. I walked over to them and said have you guys come up with a plan once we get there? huh, no Yvi said and looked at mammon, I am going over there with Loard. She smiled at me and started heading towards Loard. That was weird, so what is going on?

Mammon did not respond to me. Mammon I am talking to you, what is going on? Mammon turned to me and his eyes where dark, I changed my vision from night to regular vision and I was shocked to see them that red. Okay did I say something wrong? You are annoying, my sister and I always must get you out of messes. Wait? What? Yamaries, he said and stopped walking, looked at me and said I cannot do this anymore. You are weak, you slow us down and quite frankly your just needy. I think it is time as the king of hell you just go back and leave. I was hurt, how can you say that? We all have been through so much. I did not notice when Loard and Yvi got to us but Loard answered little miss we think it is for the best. You too, how can you say that. I looked at Yvi and she placed her head down. Do all of you feel this way? Yvi and Loard did not say anything, but Mammon did. Yes, we all do, you are too much for us to deal with right now. How could you say something like that? I felt my heart breaking, I am sorry, but I do not want to be with you any longer this was a mistake, go back home, hearing this tore me apart. Yvi, Loard lets go we must get to the third gate and kill Zozo. Wait I managed to say, you are going to rescue my grandfather, right? He looked at me and said why would I do that? I only lead you to believe that so we could get pass these gates but your beginning to be more trouble that you are worth. Tears started to flow, what is going on? Let us go, I am tired of seeing human reactions it bores me. I watched as Mammon, Loard and Yvi walked away. This overwhelming feeling of loneliness came over me, it hit me like a ton of bricks. I started to think to myself, was it something I said or did. The I realized I did not know where to go. Wait! I yelled but it was too late they were nowhere to be seen. They left me, he did not want me there and I know why. Once again, I began to cry, it is because of what I said about Yvi and maybe because I cry way too much. I never felt so alone like I did at that moment. The only person that held that small piece of hope together was gone. Now there was pure loneliness, how can someone live with this loneliness it is so painful and sad.

I started to feel a little dizzy, I brushed it off as I was tired from what just happened. I am so sleepy, if I just close my eyes and rest for a little this will all go away like a bad dream. I laid down on the floor which surprisingly felt soft. I am not sure why but as I began to close my eyes and a certain line that Mammon said flashed in my memory. "I am tired of seeing human reactions it bores me." Mammon would never say that, he would never use the word humans or bored. That is not mammon I said out loud. I struggled to get up, but I finally got to sit up. This is not real; mammon would never say something like that. Oops, SSS… I guess you figured me out. Particularly good Yamaries, you know the prince very well. I am extremely surprised that you lasted this long. Your reputation precedes you. I got up and yelled show yourself, as you wish. Everything changed from the cave back to the dark room where I was still sitting at the table. There he was half human half snake, he had hands, torso, and face of a human, but the bottom was all snake. His eyes where snake like as well. My name is Alic and I am the gate keeper of loneliness. It was necessary for me to at least taste your loneliness, but you got me before I could fully enjoy it. Now Yamaries I will let your prince and the others come through, I watched as they came into the door and walked past me. Mammon? Oh, they can't hear you, see they 'll go to gate three but you, you will stay here with me. I need your loneliness; it is to divine to let go. SSS… no this is not happing I yelled Mammon!!! Keep yelling Yamaries lets taste that loneliness, you will never be with them or your mom and dad. You belong to me, SSS.

How am I going to get out of this? I kept telling myself, come on Yamaries think, Mammon please help me. I kept telling myself not realizing that I was feeding into his desire of loneliness. Please Mammon hear me I need your help, I could see them looking at the gate and looking around. I could see Mammon mouthing something but could not make it out. Loneliness is always so tasteful when it is real. Call for him, Yamaries do you feel it the loneliness, the sadness. I did not answer, but this feeling was so unbearable honestly, I felt like dying, just to make it go away. SSS…Ha, ha this taste so good, you are by far the best, yes give in let go. No, I must fight. I have… I felt myself starting to fall asleep and everything was starting to go black. This is it, I told myself, and I guess I have reached my limit. Yes…SSS… give in to my loneliness, I just laid there in the dark alone. I was ready to give up all hope until I heard someone's voice. It was trying to say something, but I could not understand. Yam… I heard it almost sounded like Mammon, but I could not be sure. Even though I did not know who it was it gave me hope, so I started to fight. Yama… yes that is, that is Mammon, and he is looking for me. Mammon? Please do not go. Mammon can you hear me. Yamaries! NO! He roared you would stay here. SSS… you are MINE! No, I am not MAMMON! I hollered, I am not sure why or how, but he heard me, Yamaries I am coming, Endores Nocmoro. I heard him say and this bright blue light formed in his hands, but I could not tell if it was a knife or something else. I really could not tell you because just like that I passed out; I was in the dark pit of the abyss. No sound or sight, it was scary for me, I did not even dream. Yamaries wake up; I heard a sweet voice calling for me in this darkness. Yamaries please wake up. I slowly woke up from my darkness and started seeing the light. I came to, I began to blink to be able to focus my vision, and I am not sure if it was something I made up but I swear I thought I seen a silhouette of a women glowing all around her. That smile, I knew that smile. I blinked again, she was gone, and I could see Mammon, was that my mom? I felt myself start to cry; it cannot be I told myself I am not that lucky. Besides Alic put me through a lot and had me talking about them. I still could not stop myself from crying. Yamaries you are okay, I promise. Mammon thought I was crying because of what happened. I would let him think that for now. I am okay, really, I am okay Mammon. I looked around and noticed that we were around many trees, I am not sure after I battled Alic this is where he dropped us. I hope where close to the third gate, Yvi has something with Loard that might help us at least point us to the right direction. Okay, I got up slowly and told Mammon we need to go find them. We began to walk towards them, and I felt this heaviness. Mammon what is that? That is Yvi and Loard doing an incantation to help us find the third gate. Okay, I told him that makes sense. I felt like we were walking for a long time, Mammon how far we are. I feel like we have been walking a while. You are right, I had a feeling, and I think we have been going in a circle. We passed this tree twice, okay how can he see that is the same tree. So, what is going on? Something does not want us to leave, Mammon I think it does not want us to find the gate. I told Mammon I wanted to try something, if the forest only wants us to find the gate then we should as it for directions. Well, mammon said at this point what other chance do we have, go ahead, well he sounded so assuring. I closed my eyes and concentrated. Show me the gate, I said in my head. I really could not picture the gate since I never seen it before. I stood completely still, and it showed me absolutely nothing. I felt dumb; suddenly I got this flash of a tree. Really a tree! Mammon looked at me as if I were dumb. What? It showed me a tree, just a tree. Mammon looked around and noticed the marking on the tree, they looked tribal and runic combined. What do you think that means? Let us find another tree with markings it might take us to it. I searched my surrounding area never leaving Mammon out of my sight. I could not lose him again, Mammon I do not see anything, do you? He did not answer me, I looked up and he was still looking around at the trees, I guess he did not hear me. I was going to start walking over to him, but this weird noise coming from behind me caught my attention. I turned around and at first; I could not see anything but darkness. Then I heard signing like a lullaby and this blue glowing mist started to appear. I was not afraid of the mist mostly intrigued. I heard little whispers almost as if it wanted me to follow it, I called out for Mammon, but he never came. Therefore, I decided to follow the blue mist. It led me to another tree with the writing on it, the blue mist rapped itself around the tree making the marking glow. Slowly the path began to reveal itself in the form of a blue glow. Ma… I was in the middle of calling him, but he was already following, he covered my mouth and said Shh, do not say another word. If you scare it, it will not finish leading us the rest of the way. Okay, I whispered, and we followed the blue glow.

The singing was beautiful the lullaby was something that sounded so familiar, but I could not place it. Mammon whispered in my ear, be careful do not listen to close I do not want you to fall into a trans. Okay, I told him and I kept staring at the mist that guided us through the forest closer to the gate. Well I thought the blue mist was going to lead us to the gate but instead the blue mist leads us up to a girl laying on the ground, I think she was asleep. Umm, Mammon is she supposed to be here. I am not sure; she might be another lost soul. Oh well, we cannot leave, I walked over to her tapped her and said miss are you okay? She began to move, and I backed up a little, I did not want her to start doing something crazy. Hello, miss is you okay. I repeated. She opened her eyes, sat up, and looked at Mammon and me. She was the most beautiful girl I have ever seen, and I am a girl. Are you okay? She quickly looked at Mammon and smiled, okay not awkward at all. Hey, did you hear me at all or are you deaf? Oh, hello, I did not see you there, she said with this soft, sweet voice. I am fine thanks for asking. I was on my way…. She just stopped mid-sentence. On your way where? Well I cannot remember but now he is here, and I am sure he could help me find my way. Very funny, I thought to myself, I am not going to let that bother me. Well we are looking for something and we do not want to waste any more time. She jumped up and stood right next to Mammon and said can I come with; I rather lost my way. If I go with you, I will probably find my way back home. Mammon looked at me and of course, I felt bad so I said sure, you could come with us. Great Mammon know which way we go to get to the gate. A gate she replied, I remember a gate, it is this way follow me. She grabbed Mammon's hand and pulled him closer to her and down a dirt trail, which I know was not there before. I looked at Mammon with an angry face and he just looked at me confused. I keep forgetting he is a demon, but she is in infuriating me. I started to follow behind them down the path and I see miss thing giggling and learning on him as if he said something funny. We all know he cannot tell a joke. I could feel my face getting red, the next move she made I seen it in slow motion that is how angry I got. Her left hand she placed on his back and she started to go down as if towards his lower back, the right-hand laid right on top of his chest touching his peeks. I think steam was coming out of my ears. I quickly got to them to say something, if you... but she cut me off, like I said look a gate. I quickly looked up and there it was a gate, it looked as if we were in mid-evil times. It was more of a drawbridge than a gate, lucky little shit, and the gate saved her. I wonder how we will get inside. I looked over at Mammon to asked him that question, but he looked entertained by little miss perky. I cleared my throat and said are you two done? We need to figure out how to get in. Oh, she said that is easy I live here, she turned her hand up in the air flipped it over and blew on her hand and this blue dust came out and the drawbridge began to open. That is funny a minute ago she could not remember anything and now she remembers that she lives in a castle. Once the bridge came all the way down, we walked through. Funny thing about this castle there was no darkness. I felt as if I walked into someone home, welcome to my castle, my home. Okay was she rubbing her home in my face, do you live alone? I asked her. Yes, of course silly, why would not I. come let me show you the grand hall, she grabbed Mammon's hand and pulled him towards a room. I quickly walked with them, I am not leaving her alone with him, and did she just take a jab at me. She makes me angry; the grand hall was just grand and beautiful. It was something out of a fairy tale, I hate her, do you not have one of these? She asked him as she got closer. Umm, mammon can I speak with you for a moment please. I asked him, I really do try not to show my green wicked witch of the west side, but this chick is working every never. Yes, Yamaries? Can you not let her touch you like that; it makes me extremely uncomfortable? He looked at me and stared into my eyes, yes, I will make sure she does not make you uncomfortable. Thank you, now let us go see how we get to the next gate. Let us, I wonder where she went? We walked back into the grand hall and she was gone. Okay, umm…. I just realized That I do not know her name. Let me ask Mammon he looked like he must know her a little better. Mammon? I called out to him; I walked out of the grand hall and stood by the stairway where Mammon was standing at staring. What is he…I turned my head and this little hussy changed her outfit and put on the skimpiest outfit I have ever seen, and believe me I have seen some stuff? I quickly looked back at Mammon and he could not keep his eyes off. I really do not think she looks that great, come on, let me show you to the dinner table. I got my servants to start preparing, she held on to Mammon, did you get your other clothes dirty I asked her. Oh, my, I forgot you were here; yes, I was getting a little hot. She looked at me up and down and said you might want to change you look awful. We will wait for you in the dining area, No, you will not I told her, I am fine just like this and I do not need to eat, we must go. You are always in such a hurry. How did she know I am always in a hurry? I think I know who she is come Mammon lets head to the dining room. I felt my jealousy rise; Mammon looked as though he was going to go with her. I was going to stop him and yell, but I had a feeling that is all part of her game. If I give into jealousy where stuck it must be his choice. Mammon? I called out I am not staying I am leaving; I must find the next gate and I must get back to Loard and Yvi. It is your choice if you would like to come with or stay. Clever little human you figured it all out, they did say you were smart and witty. You see Yamaries I am Zona and my love dust is the strongest no man has ever chosen someone besides me.

I laughed Zona you must not know; Mammon and I are as one. So good luck, I hope I told myself. Well you are right about one thing Zona said it is his choice. Yamaries, I…he began to trail off. Mammon are you okay. Of course, he is why would not he be. Please stop talking to me and stop cheating, I know you are still using that dust, you could hurt him. Oh, please he is the king oh hell he could sustain anything, I am sorry Mammon, but right now it is up to you. You must fight, if you do not, I will have no choice but to leave you behind. I am so sorry Yamaries… I felt my heart drop, I looked over at her, she was smiling, and she leaned over and laid her head on his chest. I closed my eyes and felt the tears flowing down my face; I guess it is not as strong as I thought. I turned around and began to walk towards the front door. DO not be sad sweetie no man has ever left my castle. True love is a myth for hopeless dreamers. Good Luck out there you are going to need it. I wanted to snap and kick her little prissy ass, but then we will lose. So instead, I will suck it up and take an L for the team. Yamaries! Wait! I turned around, Mammon quickly drew his sword and placed it across her neck and said next time do not underestimate your foe. I knew exactly who you were since the forest I ate a certain leaf that counter acts your little dust, I just needed to keep up the rouse. What? I said to myself, why he could not tell me that. I am so sorry Yamaries I had to look convincing or she would has caught on. I smiled; you are good I told him. He turned to Zona and said you will show us the way to the next gate, and you will release Loard and Yvi. She knew they would recognize her, so she trapped them, aren't I right Zona? I guess that means you lost, I told her. Well, well king you must have learned some new trick from the humans, who would have guessed it. Unfortunately, I am bound to this stupidity of losing or winning, so yes, I will show you where the other gate is. No, I said very quickly I knew she might come up with another little trick and I am not falling for that. You will take us to the gate all four of us, you will release Loard and Yvi right in front of the gate as well. Sneaky little white witch, you are particularly good at catching on to our tricks. As you wish, come this way she said. Umm are you going to let me go? I cannot take you there if my head is cut off now can I. Mammon threw back is sword but placed it on her back, this is insurance he said. That made me laugh he almost sounded human, fine quickly this way, I do not want anyone to know what has happened. She started taking us through a hallway and down some stairs. The s lead down to some dark tunnels, if I ever were stuck in here, I would never get out it was a labyrinth. The Tunnels got darker, I could barely see them, and they were just outlining to me. I closed my eyes and opened them again to get night vision; I noticed that she was trying to do something to Mammon like try to hurt him. I lost my cool raised my hand up and out came this bright purple sword and I swung it and plunged it right in her chest on the right side. Mammon looked incredibly surprised; do not lay a hand on him because next time I will chop your head off. I quickly pulled my sword out of her and watched her heal. Mammon asked quickly how did you know that she would heal? Umm... I did not I said I really did not think it through. I smiled at him nervously, Yamaries we could have been stuck here. Yes, I know that I thought about that once it was too late. Please do not be mad, it was not the left side. Yamaries she does not have a heart, oh yeah, ha looks at that I forgot that too. He looked furious at me but look at Zona and roared get upkeep moving. We are wasting time, I kind of felt bad for her he roared at her because he was angry at me. We got to this opening and there were these purple stone that was the same color as my sword. This lite the rest of the way there I could not believe how beautiful it was and this bimbo gets to live on top of it. It is not as great as it looks, she said out loud as if she knew what I was thinking. I did not say anything I told her; no, you did not have to I could see it in your eyes. It gets boring after a millennium or two. Be quite mammon told her as if annoyed still. It is up a head she told him; you do not have to get ugly. I need my sister back and Loard they better be there when we get to the gate. Yes, they are already there. Mammon I called for him, you are mad at me stop taking it out on her it is not fair. FAIR! He roared fair is you are always acting without thinking getting all of us hurt or placing our lives at stake. Okay, where did that come from, Okay I am sorry it is hard not to when you and the other are too afraid to quickly act. Mammon roared, are you out of your mind, I have been planning and fighting wars before you were thought of so do not question my choices. That was hurtful, now you will follow me and stay quiet. We finally got to the gate and I could see Loard and Yvi, I quickly ran to them passing Mammon and Zona. Yvi quickly got into battle stands and said Yamaries get behind me this tricky little mink has tricks under her sleeves. Oh no, Yvi she led us down here, oh did she now. That is the first, huh? Just like that Loard pulled out his sword and so did Yvi. What is going on? My brother is under a spell, huh? I turned to look at Mammon who's eyes where bright red. Now my queen shall we kill them all, yes, my king but leave the little human to me. She gets on my nervous, I could not believe it, everything flipped, and I see everything in slow motion. What is happening, my thoughts where everywhere and I was so focus in them that I did not noticed Zona jumping into midair ready to place her sword in my chest. I am not sure what really happened, but I blinked turned towards her pulled my hand out and the purple sword appeared, with one swift move and no knowledge of how I did it, I chopped off her head. Mammon Hollard NO! my queen and fell to the ground. Her body laid in one spot and her head in another, I was covered in black goo. Mammon got up his eye's bright red, it looked a little brighter than before and started to charge at me. Yvi quickly clocked him over the head and knocked him out. I was in shock; it was that easy for him to forget his love for me. Yvi walked over to me and said he was not himself; she is more powerful than you will ever know. Look behind you, I turned around and her head and body where missing. She cannot die Loard continued but she is scared and hurt now that she is defeated and you little miss are one strong competitor. Loard, Yvi I know I was, but I thought he was to. I understand little miss, come let us get the master and open this gate. Loard and Yvi picked up Mammon and carried him closer to the gate. This gate looked just like first gate except in red. A bright red in fact, I wonder what tomfoolery where going to get into in here. I looked over at Yvi what should we do? I asked her since her brother thinks I act before, I think. Well honestly Yamaries we have been following you, great now I do not know what to do. I felt myself getting angry and suddenly the gates start to open. I ran closer to Loard and Yvi and said was that supposed to happen. Yvi looked at me and said no. Once the gate opened you could see red dirt or sand, should we walk through? I asked. Well we have no choice, Yvi said and began the walk through the gate. Let us try not to get separated please Yvi said. I sort of took that as a jab towards me bit I did not say anything and kept on moving. It felt as if we were walking through this sand for hours and it was getting hot. Yvi I think we might need to slow down and rest. No, she snapped at me, we need to keep moving. Do you even know where we are going? We need to stop and get out barring together. Fine! Let us stop so the princess could get some rest, Really, she went there. I thought we were over that now; I could feel myself getting angry, but I swallowed it up. I looked around to see if I could find an opening or cave something with shade. At first, I thought I was seeing things like a mirage, but I started squinting and with hesitation I said I found one. Yvi looked at me annoyed and said what did you find? Look I think it a cave, let us go to it. Yvi turned around and looked in the direction that I was pointing at and said alright Loard lets go to the cave our future queen has spoken. That made my blood boil, the whole walk there I kept my mouth shut because I knew that it was going to get ugly. Once we got into the cave, we all started to look around separately and made a circle straight to the middle, Loard spoke out and said I will go find something to start a fire. I hear it gets cold out here, well if the princess would not have asked us to stop, we might have made it to the next gate. Loard stood there awkwardly and he gently laid Mammon down and started to walk away. Listen Yvi I do not have to listen to your crap, where supposed to be doing this together. Oh really! She snapped back you have been trying to lead the way since we passed the first gate and that is my brethren's job not yours. I have not Yvi and besides, we have made it this far because of me. No, you got us out of messes you got us in the first place. I felt my face get red and my ears where on fire. Listen!!! You and Mammon do not have to be here, I could manage on my own. While everyone is twilling their thumbs, I am making moves so kiss my ... Mammon moaned and we both turned to look at him. Brother

Yvi responded first, Are you okay? Really, I said to myself, of course not Yvi, you knocked him upside his head he probably has a headache. I did it to save you, from another situation you placed us in. Listen here you do not have to follow me, STOP! Loard roared you two are driving me insane. We need to stop feeding into what it wants, Yvi turned around looked at Loard and said what are you talking about? She had this snooty tone to it. Do not talk to him like that. Yamaries, Loard called do not we need to get it together. There is no god here to guard these gates just a creature who will not show itself but can manipulate and eat us. The more we fight amongst ourselves the closer it will get to us and kill us so, lets calm down relax. It is getting dark let us start this fire. Fine, I said, I got up and help Loard with the sticks, while Yvi took care of Mammon. Little Mis being mad at the master also counts, I looked at Loard but could not get mad at him. I know Loard your right. I will go get more sticks that will distract me. Do not wander to far little miss, whatever inhabits these caves I do not think it is gone. What? Wait? Huh, are we going to get eaten two ways? Loard laughed no little mis it was a jest. There is no other creature here, Really! Loard I cannot with you. I started to laugh, and he said but that is an opening for the creature to come through and kill us if it hears us fighting. That is another joke, right? Oh no, this one is true. I quickly got close to Loard and said we have enough sticks to keep us warm through the night. I smiled and went to go start the fire.

As the fire was going, I sat at one side Yvi, Loard and Mammon who was finally up on the other. Mammon looked over at me and did not say one word he did not even apologize. He sure was very talkative to his sister and Loard. I looked around to see where I could lay my head, I started to make a sand pillow. It was slightly soft but getting rid of the sand in my hair is going to be well we all know. Loard looked over at me and said rest well little mis, I will be keeping watch. Thank you Loard, you are the best. I rubbed that in mammon's face. I laid down and closed my eyes, I did not think I was tired, but I feel asleep quickly. I never thought I could dream but I did that night. I dreamed that I was laying on the grass in front of that old house that had the oldest portal. I sat up and looked around, I could see two bright lights. I was not afraid of it I was filled with joy. I Stood up as the light got closer and I could see clearly what was coming towards me. I could not believe it, I began to cry, it was both my parents. They look exactly as I remember them "Mom, Dad I said is that really you? They smiled and I ran to them and held them. This cannot be real; I could hold you and touch you. I have missed you so much I said to them, we have also missed you honey, my mom said. My dad kissed me on the forehead and said you look just like your mother, lucky you. I laughed and said dad I miss your corny jokes. Yamaries listen we came here to tell you something. Okay, that turned quickly, yes mom what is going on? You must choose they both said. What? Mom what are you guys talking about? You must choose; this is all they kept saying. Little mis? I heard my name and my parents disappeared. I awoke with Loard in my face. Little mis are you alright? You have been crying. Huh? I wiped my eyes and noticed I have been crying, oh Loard it is nothing. Are we ready to go? Yes, the master and Yvi are outside ready. Wow, they wasted no time at all. I got up brushed off the sand and walked outside. Where going to head do west until we see a big opening that is where the fifth gate lies, Mammon said. He did not once look at me, okay fine whatever. Yvi started walking a long side Mammon and Loard was right next to me. Loard, do you think I am trying to take the lead? Little mis, you are letting this place get to you. Do you not see that the master and little Misses are being influenced by the creature? Master was already weakened and Misses well she hates the world, quite literally. So, she is an easy target but you little mis you are a little harder to crack, therefore all the other creatures and gods let you go and did what you asked. It is no secret that you are special, and they know it. You are a fighter and that is something we all need. Thank you Loard I needed to hear that. Anytime little mis and please do not forget that. Yvi turned around and said what are you planning? Brother, she stopped these two have been chatty back here, while you are hard at work finding our way. Really you… Remember little mis what I told you. I quickly took a deep breath, Yvi nobody is planning anything, we cannot walk all day in silence now can we, so, we decided to conversate. You and your human ways are going to kill us, okay what am I supposed to keep quiet to. It is a long walk it goes faster when you speak. Quite you two Mammon said, I just felt the ground move. I looked over at Loard and he nodded in agreeance. Oh crap, it found us, Mammon what do we do? Oh, Yvi said now you want to listen to my brother. Yvi shut up, right now is not the time, as I was going to say something else to Yvi I felt the ground shake. I panicked a little bit; Mammon say something quick I said to myself. He looked over at us and said RUN! We all took off behind Mammon, I kept looking behind us and seen the ground going up. Guys we must move faster it is right behind us. Yvi quickly responded, we are moving as fast as we can. You are picking the bad times to argue girl, just move I said to Yvi. It felt like I was in an earthquake when the creature came out of the ground. It looked like something out of the movies, it had two heads one dragon and the other a snake. The body was snake, the dragon let out the biggest noise that rattled our hearing and our vision. We all fell to the ground and I could hear Mammon hollering we have to keep moving. I shook it off and got up, I grabbed Loard and kept on moving. I did not look back I just ran. I ran until I finally seen an opening a noticeably big one. It was the size of spaceship, I got excited Loard we made it. We both went into the big opening that was a cave and took some deep breaths. I was so out of shape, Loard are you okay? Yes, little mis I am fine. I sucked it up and said Mammon, Yvi are you guys okay? But they did not respond. I looked around and noticed it was just me and Loard. Loard I said in a panic I think they are still out there. We both ran towards the opening but was pushed back by a force field. I flung me down on my butt, I looked at Loard and said what the hell was that? I am not sure little mis, but I think it does not want us to leave. The master and little misses are on their own. No, Loard I just cannot leave them, I got up and ran up to the opening again and it once again flung me away. Little mis Loard said, they must let go of their anger. They both must work together, or they will die. Loard I said I must help them, Little mis they must do it alone. For the first time I felt helpless, I cannot lose him Loard, Little mis I know you love the master, but somethings he will have to learn on his own. Sooner or later he will have to make the biggest decision of his life and no one is going to make it for him. Loard what are you talking about? I was so confused on his answer, I swear it felt like he knew something I did not. Little mis come sit down here with me and get a fire started, the creature cannot come in here, for this is the path to the fifth gate. We will be safe, Loard it is not us that I am worried about. I know little mis, I know, I sat down next to Loard and leaned in to lay on him, there, there little mis it will be alright. I have faith in my master and misses they are stronger than you think.

It felt like an eternity that they were out there, but it was thirty minutes when I heard hurry Yvi, it was Mammon I got so excited to hear his voice that I quickly got up and ran to him. I got to him and gave him a huge and I said I was so worried, and I am glad you both made it through. I let him go and looked at him, he did not look amused. Oh, I am so sorry I did not mean to, I will just go back and sit down. Loard he said how could you not come out and help us? Master there is a barrier and we could not get out. Why you... Loard quickly got up and Hollard at both Yvi and Mammon, Encanto Mora and they both fell to their knees and covered their eyes. Loard, what did you do? I took off the enchantment. These two clearly have a lot of work to do. Mammon was the first to respond, Loard what is going on? Master you were under an immensely powerful spell. I feel like my head is about to explode Mammon said, well master you were under that spell for a while so I do believe it will have that effect on you. Yvi started to come to, Mammon what happened? I feel like a dragon ran me over. Yes, misses.... Oh, for crying out loud I said yes both of you were under a powerful spell and Loard took it off so get yourself together. Loard looked at me he smiled and said well little mis it looks like you need some work done too. Huh? Come, he grabbed my hand and sat me down and said Encanto Mora and just like that my anger was gone and I began to throw up. I felt dizzy, this felt like the worse hangover ever, I promise not to drink again, is all I could say in between my vomiting. There, there little mis it will pass, it took about twenty minutes for it to pass. We started to get up and move a little bit and we just stared at each other; it was awkwardly silent. I decided to break the silence and spoke out, I am so sorry I didn't mean to hurt anyone's feelings, I did not mean anything I said you guys are my family... Mammon cut me off and said Yamaries

I apologize you just did what anyone would do if they were being attacked. Yvi did not say anything, Yvi I especially want to apologize to you I feel like you have been the one I picked on the most, I said. Yvi turned to me and said Yamaries do not. Do not apologize everyone here has said and acted foolish and we are embarrassed. I forgive each one of you, same here I said. Mammon smiled we are family and we will get through these gates together. Wow I said to myself that was cheese. I smiled and we pushed on through the cave. I hope this gate is not going to give us these many problems. I am not sure how much more we could take.

We finally got to the gate, well actually it was a door, like a regular door to a home. The door was a mustard colored, okay this is so weird. Who knew going through these gates was going to be weird like the twilight zone? Once again, we were all staring at the door, thinking I am quite sure on how we are going to get it open. Mammon got closer to the door and it flew open. He looked at us and said this is going to be a crazy ride. I did not like the sound of that. We all braced ourselves and walked right through that door to the unknown.

<u>*Chapter Nine*</u>

s we walked through the door, the room we entered looked just like my home in Chicago. Okay, what is going on? I said out loud. Do you recognize this place? Mammon asked, yes this is my old home in Chicago, it looks just like I last saw it. Welcome to my home Yamaries, I wanted you to feel comfortable, for me. Okay, I know this is going to sound weird but why do these god's have it out for me. I have never done anything to them. What do you want with her? Mammon quickly responded. Well this is different she said, and I got dizzy after she said that, and the room began to change, it looked like the castle from gate three. Oh no I have a bad feeling about this, I told myself. Normally humans are the ones that harbor so much guilt but you king of hell, you have a lot it and it is so tasty. She came out of the dark and she was half woman and half dragon. Her face was a woman's face with dragon eyes, her teeth pointy as a needle and her hands where long and scaly, her finger nails a tar black color. She had dragon feet and a tail. She was not scary, but pretty she was not neither. Come king let us have a sit in the grand hall do you remember the grand hall, king of hell? Leave him alone, why are you doing this to him? I am the one you want. Oh, please it is not always about you, oh hero have a seat and be quiet. Yvi grabbed me and whispered do not confront her, she will hurt him. Once she has her fix on someone that is all she could think about. We must wait and see how new are going to get through this. Do you Remember anything about that gate with Zora? Yes, but I am not enormously proud of the way I acted. No, not you my brother, Yvi said. Umm, well…. I was too afraid to answer because honestly, I was so invested in my emotions with Zora that I did not pay attention to his. Yvi I … I started to feel guilty for just thinking about myself. I am so sorry I ca does not remember.

Okay, Lets follow her lead. We all got to the grand hall and it was a little different then the empty room Zora showed us. There was a long table with chairs. There was food on the table and pretty china as well. Everyone sit, let us eat, we all grabbed a seat close to each other, she sat at the end of the table I sat on her right and Mammon sat in front of me on her left. Yvi sat next to me and Loard next to Mammon. She giggled and said my, my this really is a close group. Loard looked at her and said Lucinda what do you want with my master? Lucinda, so that is her name I said to myself. How does Loard know her? I have a lot of questions. Oh, Loard it has been a while has it. You still look ravaging as usual. Gage, she thought he is hot, oh god I think I just throw up in my mouth. That was his old squeeze, I get it. What do you want with my master? Loard was straight to the point and did not acknowledge her comment. I grabbed me some mash potatoes and chicken and waiting for the show, I knew this was going to be good. Oh, Loard always so serious, no time for play. Always the lap dog, you are so boring, always chasing your master and no guilt, no wonder I let you go. I was going to say something but, Yvi held my arm and shook her head. Fine, I knotted, it was fine at first but now it was getting out of control. Lucinda, I will not ask again. SILENCE! You are in my realm now, and I make the rules. Now, my sweet king of hell shall we talk about your and Zora little shall I say... and she began to giggle again. That really struck a nerve with me, fling she finished, you know king I think she really did have a little thing for you. Well now king who would not have a thing for you so handsome. She caressed his face with those long black nails. Mammon grabbed her hand and said say what you like but do not touch me and his eyes turned reed. There he is the king, yes let us begin. Mammon who was quiet at first began to speak, there is nothing to tell, I was under a spell. Now sweet king does not lie, you will feel much better if you just lay it all on the table. Mammon looked at her and said, there is nothing to talk about so let us move on. You really are a stubborn one, aren't you? Or is it that you do not want to tell your sweet hero the truth. I looked at Mammon, but he did not make eye contact with me. You are no fun king, but you are the tastiest. Well hero I guess I will go to you but make no mistake king if you want to pass and go to the next gate you will have to give me what I want. Shall we move to the living room. Yamaries you remember the living room, don't you? My heart dropped; I remember that living room like if it was yesterday. She got up from the table and walked out, we all started to get up and I called for mammon. Hey are you okay? He did not respond. Do not let her get to you. He finally looked at me and said, she will never get to me. Then he walked away and exited the grand hall. I looked at Yvi and Loard they both had their head down and said nothing. Let us go Yvi finally said, we all walked out and ended straight into my old living room. I wanted to run, but I knew to get out of here I will have to tell it all. She was standing in front of the couches and told us to come and sit without looking at us. We walked over to the couch and sat down, are we ready to play little hero? I hate when she calls me that. Yes, I am ready, Now do you remember the night your father died, please do not, can you pick another day and time I felt guilty. I have plenty, yes little hero but this one, aww this one is the tastiest, this is the one I carve. Please, I cannot, yes, I smell it little hero, tell everyone what happen two hours before you found out of your father's death. The pain that came rushing in was so unbearable, that is okay little hero lets I'll take you there shall we, she moved out the way and it was like watching a movie and someone hit replay. I am coming down the hall, dad you promised you will be here to watch the movie with me. Dad you always work late, you said you are going to be different, FINE! Whatever do not come home at all. I hung up the phone and came into the living room. Oh god, I killed my father. I started to cry, the tears where flowing. Ding, Dong, NO PLEASE STOP! Why little hero? Please stop. It is your fault your dad left the office to come be with you. If you would have been a good girl and let him be, he would still be with you. It was a mistake, I did not mean for him to die, I was angry. I just wanted him to be with me. Yes, oh so sweet it tastes so good. Mammon got up Lucinda enough leave her be. Oh, sweet king shall we move on to you? No, she growled, fine but remember yours is the one I want. Yvi shall we continue with you? Come let us go to the playroom. Playroom? I thought as I was wiping my tears away. We all stood up but Yvi. Loar4d and mammon walked to the next room, I stood behind to get Yvi. Yvi what is wrong? I cannot face that. Huh? What do you mean? He will never forgive me. Who are you talking about? She did not answer, she just got up and walked into the next room. I quickly followed and it was literally a child's playroom meant for demons. The walls where black with black carpet and red furniture. The kids' toy where all in a corner wall nice and neat. I looked over at mammon and his eyes where blank, he was expressionless, not that is weird but lately he has been giving emotions. Since there is no seat here let me bring some, she waved her hand and chairs rose from the bottom of course they were red. Sit everyone, let us go down memory lane. Here at the Morning Star family residence, now Yvi are we going to be willing to share or shall I just play the scene for you? Yvi did not say anything she looked so conflicted, fine you are just like your brother. Let us see aww yes let us begin here. Just like that little Yvi came into the playroom. Stupid brother of mine, he always gets all the attention. I hate him, I wish he were never born first. I looked over at Yvi who was not looking at all. I wonder what she did that could have been so bad. Well little Yvi said he will not be the favorite for long and she smiled. She went over to Mammon's cubby to get one of his toys, brethren's favorite toy passed down from dad's dad god himself. She walked over to the fireplace and smiled. Then within seconds there was a small explosion, little Yvi jumped back looked around and ran out the door. Along came Little Mammon and was looking around, he quickly walked over to the fireplace and noticed that his favorite toy was have burned. Oh NO! did is going to kill me, as soon as he said that along came in lucifer the most handsome of men. He is so young and muscular; Mammon looks just like him. Mammon, what are you doing? No dad it was not me. You liar, I entrusted you with that toy it had magical elements from my father, Dad! Whack! Whack! Lucifer slapped and slapped Mammon until he began to bleed. I could not help but cry, how can he be so mean. Little Mammon started to cry, STOP! Your crying the men in this family do not cry. You are useless just like your mother, he walked out of the room and this woman walks in she was not hideous, but she was not ugly either. She had long black hair two small horns on her forehead with yellow cat eyes. Mammon sweetheart come, she held him and wiped away his blood. I hate him mom, oh my that is his mom. No, Mammon you do not, your father misses his father and that was the only thing he had from up there, that is all. One day mom little Mammon said, dad will pay. That is my little warrior she hugged him and from the corner of the door little Yvi was watching. The little Yvi looked so scared and guilty but never said anything, she just ran to her room. Funny Lucinda said even in hell the kids act like humans, so full of emotions. Oh, what is this? I smell that guilt Yvi and I am in love with it. Yvi got up quickly from her chair and charged at Lucinda, I was going to reach for her, but she is quick. Out of nowhere Mammon blocked his sister who already had her sword drawn. Everything happened so quickly, sister he said, sit and do not move again. How dare you draw your sword at me, Lucinda said with rage. I should… Mammon cut her off, you should do absolutely nothing and continue these charades. I keep the place and order here, now there is the big bad king of hell, but you know what here in my realm you are not. She leaned closer to him and said Zozo is and she smiled. Mammon's eyes got red a very bright red. How dare you talk to my master that way, Loard got up and roared and with that his hands flew up and he yelled "Noctora Uminos" and Lucinda was quickly bound to the ground with her arm's spread out. Why you insolent little… this has gone far enough, you will release us to the next gate, or I will force it out of you. You could try my love man, but we both know you cannot because you still love me. Loard moved his hands and said, "Lunas Naras" and Lucinda began to scream. Would you like to try this again? Fine, I will show you. You must let me go; I cannot open a portal to the next gate bound. Oh, Lucinda you are still so funny. We both know you can with three little words only you can say. She looked surprised as if he were not supposed to know that. "Zentora Acraba… she stopped mid spell, King do yourself a favor before you get all nasty inside I would tell the little hero why you feel so guilty, some advice from someone who failed at love. Enfinito, she finished, and a door appeared. Mammon walked over to the door and opened it, there it was the sixth gate, it was black, and I think there was fog coming from it. He turned to her and said I will never be like you, oh but my king I could smell the rot of guilt and trust festering inside you. Mammon looked at me and Yvi and said go through we will be right behind you. Okay I said. I grabbed Yvi and walked through, the sixth gate scared me, the fog came from inside the gate and the gate was huge and black. I got a little closer and seen that the gate had webs on it. That is lining from a soul that passes through, I jumped, and the gate opened. Mammon talked to me, that was a miracle we both moved back as the gate opened. I thought they were webs was all I could say. It was very dark, umm guys this is creepy. I see Yvi and Loard walk right in as if nothing they must be used to the dark. I walked through to and I ended up at a graveyard, I looked around and noticed I was alone, Loard? Yvi? I kept looking around Mammon. Someone please answers me. I began to panic a little, Hello Yamaries, a man's voice came from my left. Hello? Who are you? Well I am the keeper of the gate of fear. I looked around and was looking at all the gravestones, where are you at gatekeeper? No, No said a man in a black suit with a black top hat and a cane with a skull at the end. He came out from behind one of the gravestones. I am not the keeper of gate six but the gate of fear., you little Yamaries are going to give me your biggest fear. Where is everyone else? Do not worry about them it is about you here, they have their own fears to battle. You have us all facing our fears, how can you be here and there at the same time? He laughed I am not what I appear to be. I can take any form I choose. You little Yamaries, like the human expression says, you wear your fear on your sleeves. He stood there staring at me with the creepiest smile, but it was more of a blank stare then suddenly, he twitched. Shall, I show you he said. Okay, I said nervously, and he snapped his finger. I was looked around and noticed that I was right back at that stupid castle, crap! I said he looked at me and laughed. I am never going to be able to get rid of this castle or the owner I said to myself. Why are we here? I said to him annoyingly. Your biggest fear of course, he said with a smile. Very funny I do not fear her, No, no, not her this watch. Mammon is standing at the bottom of the steps and Zora is coming down the stairs, she was wearing a wedding dress. Wait! I yelled everything stood still like if I pressed pause on my PlayStation 4 remote. This will never happen I do not fear this, no he said slowly looking at me deeply, you are right but let it play out. She started to walk down the stairs again and Mammon said you look beautiful in that dress. Oh, Mammon thank you. You know it should have been you I was going to marry. Yes, but I choose Yamaries, oh king you should tell her the truth we are supposed to be together. My heart began to race, choose Mammon right now me or her. Why, please stop and everything froze. Why are you doing this? I want your fear, I is not that obvious, yours is good but his is better.

Wait, What?! He showed me a glimpse of Mammon's fear was, why her I was furious. Oh, little Yamaries have fun tout a l'heure, a hole opened, and I feel right through. I landed in something soft almost like grass. I looked around and I was back at the cemetery. I thought I was done, he could not get a fear from me, but I am right back where I started. Hey, I thought you were going to send me to the next gate? Ha, ha I never said I was going to drop you off at the gate. I said I will let you go. See your fear is a lie, your fear is something more and you will find it and only when you do, I will give you one of your comrades. Happy Searching Yamaries, oh I almost forgot some of my friends will be coming soon and they do not do well with outsiders. Bye, bye, and he was gone. I was left in this creepy cemetery, I just realized I am alone again, quick Yamaries think. I looked around to see where I could go but all I seen was gravestones. I decided to start walking to see if I could find a road or a house something. It was so quite in the graveyard; I could hear myself breathing. I am not sure why but as I walked, I decided to look at the names on the gravestones, I guess curiosity got me as I looked at one in a glance. I came to a complete stop because it took me off guard. The gravestone had Lilian Gonzalez, which is my mother's name, wait what is going on here. I looked at the gravestone next to it and it has Julian Gonzalez which is my father's name. Why are my parent's tombstone here? I felt the ground start to tremble a little. I brushed it off and keep on looking down the tombstones the next one had Juan Gonzalez, grandpa? What is going on? The ground trembled again this time I had to hold on to the tombstone. Okay, I said to myself. Hello, is someone there? I do not know what possessed me to say that, but I did. Nothing, everything went silent, I looked around and there was a thick fog starting to head my way. Am I in a scene of a horror movie, I shifted my eyes side to side just in case I see something from the corner of my eyes but there was nothing only gravestones? I moved on to the next gravestone and it had Anastasia Gonzalez. Oh, wait! What?! No what is going on, what are you playing at? Now do you see

Yamaries? He said. See what, you little shit. I was angry and ready to roar, then one of the gravestones began to glow, as if there was a light shining on it. I hesitated at first because I had a bad feeling about it, but I ignored my better judgement and walked over to the gravestone. I just stood there in front of this gravestone and right on queue I began to cry, just started whaling. The name on the gravestone was none other than Juana Gonzalez my grandmother, I felt this overwhelming feeling of loneliness. He has done it, I said to myself he figured it out my biggest fear. That is, it Yamaries you are afraid to be left alone in this world. He was right I was afraid of being the one in my family left alive, I love it! he yelled there is nothing tastier than someone's true fear. Funny your little king of hell is not so much scared of losing family. He is more afraid of you finding out something. The guy came out from behind a gravestone again. You my dear are a very quick learner. It takes humans forever to figure it out, they normally end up being eaten by my creatures. I like you, but I did say I was going to give you one of your comrades back did not I. Well my word is true he said and waved his cane. The ground began to tremble and from the ground a skinny pale hand popped out and I hear this weird moaning sound. I got closer to look and realized that was Loard's hand I quickly ran up to him and started to dig him out. Loard! Hold on, I am going to get you out. It felt like hours before I was able to get his face out of the dirt. What? He said almost done this will not due, let see how fast you are while my friends come to play. He raised his cane and slammed it against the ground, it trembled so hard I lost my balance and feel right next to Loard's hole. Lil Mis are you okay? Loard said, yeah, I just lost my balance, I looked up to see where he went but instead a hand popped up from the ground. It was in the decaying process slimy and partial bone.

YUCK! Loard we are going to have to move faster. What is it Lil mis? Believe me my friend you do not want to know, I got up quickly and began to dig out Loard as fast as I could , mind you I was digging with my hands no shovel, I dug and dug until I was able to get his arm free, I said quickly Loard you are going to have to pull yourself out of that whole. Wiggle or something, the creatures from the undead are staring to reveal their ugly faces. Every time something would pop out of the dirt from those creatures, I panicked Loard hurry up please. Lil mis I am doing my best I think I might be caught on something down here. Here give me your hands, I started to pull him out, but was only able to slowly get him out. Loard you are going to have to wiggle a little to loosen the dirt around you. Loard looked at me very confused, oh crap, Loard I am sorry move side to side. I glanced up and noticed that the creatures where gone, almost as if they disappeared. This is not good, I said out loud. Lil mis you need to tell me what is going on, the creatures Loard the creatures are all gone. Lil mis that does not sound particularly good, no it sure does not Loard we need to hurry I do not want to know where they are hiding at. I began to pull Loard out with all my strength, I was tugging and pulling I thought at one point I was going to pass out. Finally, with one last pull Loard came right out and I landed on the ground again. I looked over at Loard and started laughing, but my victory was cut short when I looked at Loard's face and his eyes looked as if he is seeing something terrifying and he is a Demon, so you know. Loard, I was so afraid to ask but I knew, what is it? He did not answer he just kept staring at whatever it was. I turned around slowly, I quickly turned around and jumped up and yelled Loard get up we must move. I grabbed Loard and we began to run. The undead where quick, which is always a cliché to me since they are dead and all. We ran as fast as we could, and I was trying to keep Loard in eyes view as well. I was at full speed looking over at Loard and I began to look forward I noticed one of the slimy undead coming for us. Loard! I yelled Run faster! As I was yelling the undead and I collided and we both landed on the ground. Lil Mis No! Loard stopped and started to run towards me. No Loard go! but before he could he got tackled down as well. We were swarmed with the undead. They were taking chunks of my soul that defiantly felt like skin. Just like that everything froze, He, he now Mammon that is the fear I am looking for. You are not always going to be able to save her. Mammon's eyes changed bright red, his winds flew open and he let out the biggest roar. If she dies you will no longer exist. Now, now little king you really should not get like that down here is my domain and little angel, demon, man really does not scare me much. Your father tried that as well, so you see how that turned out. Oh, and little king I would think hard about your title. I do not think that is your just yet, little king I think I have something more terrifying than losing your little angel Yamaries.

He lifted his cane and waved his hands; there he was Lucifer his image appeared before Mammon. I will tell you what little prince why I do not let you and your beloved go to the next gate. The Keeper of that gate is so lucky their going to have so much fun with you. Hmm, maybe he will let me watch? He has been sort of devilish lately. Oh, little prince no punt intended. He, he, he giggled, and he looked so malicious when he was talking to mammon. What do think little prince? And for hell sake calm down, you could put away your wings. How do I know what you are saying is true? Mammon said, Geez, little prince gives me credit I might be the keeper of fear, but I would never lie. There is no need when the fear of truth is so delicious, he said this as he was licking his lips. Mammon just started at him, oh you bore me, here let me show you how much of a liar I am. Oh, and prince I will see you soon, he, he. He snapped his fingers and we all landed on dirt. I got up and started to look around to see where we landed. I noticed that we were on a dirt road. I slowly started to rotate, and I saw this big old broke down eighteenth-century home. It had a decaying gate and the house was surrounded by dirt instead of grass. I looked down at mammon who was still trying to get us. Mammon look I told him, He got up and stared at the house. He still was expressionless, but Yvi spoke and said why are we at this house? I quickly looked over at her and she had this expression as if she seen a ghost. What is going on? Yvi you look like you seen something from you past. Yes, something we all have been trying to forget. I turned back to look at the house and I swear I heard the house breath. This house gives me the crept, I said out loud and it should little mis for this house is where pure evil was born. Huh? Pure evil? Yes, I will spare you the story little mis because I have a feeling you are going to hear or see it for yourself. Should we go inside? I walked up to the decaying gate and went to push it open but when I tried to open the gate it would not budge. Umm, guys we have a problem this gate will not open. Mammon walked over to the gate and said because this gate has nothing to do with you. Mammon grabbed the gate and opened it. This hard wind came bursting out along with a foul odor of hundreds of decaying bodies. I gauged I thought I was going to throw up and then I remembered I did not have a stomach. Mammon what is that smell? That is the smell of your worst nightmare, a voice came from inside the house. The voice was soft and high pitched, come in my friends come in. Unlike my fellow friends on gates on thru six I great mines at my door. I tried to look inside the door, but I could not see anything. Loard did you see the door ever open? No little mis, but here in the depts of hell things like this is not unusual. Well that is good to know, Mammon, Yvi and Loard started to walk through and right when I was going to walk in, I felt a swoop go by from above. I quickly looked up but could not see anything but pure darkness. I shrugged my shoulders and walked through the gate. It is funny but instead of walking down the walkway I walked right into the house. Can you believe this house was beautiful in the inside? Why does that always happen, welcome he said welcome, would you like something to drink? It has been a long time since I had to host visitors. Souls never ever make it this far, but prince you are not just anybody now are you. Oooo, that just makes me tingle all over, Umm, I know you are new at this, but the host always speaks to their guests face to face. Are you going to show yourself? Aww sweet Yamaries, well rude. I will show myself when I am descent. Now rude little girl goes and have a sit. Goody, Goody souls like you bore me. Mammon touched my shoulder and whispered in my ear; I do not think this gate has to do with you. I have a feeling we made it this far for a reason. Let us handle this, but mammon I began to say, NO listen to me very carefully right now arguing is not what I need just listen and follow. I was a little hesitant, but I agreed. I wonder what is going on, I know he knows something I do not.

Yvi came up to my other side and said we are going to need your attention to details. You are good in seeing things that others do not. This is what he means. The focus is on my brother which is good because your eyes is what we really need right now. Wow, I said to myself she is being nice and involved with me in their plans. Okay I whispered. Yamaries,

Yvi said we are counting on you, if you see anything out of the extraordinary or out of place, even and underlining of a sentence give us a sign. Umm, okay what sign? I am sure we will now. You have my word, I walked behind Yvi and Loard and just listen and observed. Now that she is placed where she belongs prince my guest of honor shall we enter the main hall where we all could get comfortable and chat. Oh, prince I am not sure if your little rude girl and your pet should come into my main hall. I do not want to clean afterwards. No, he did not I should slap the ignorance out his ass. I was going to say something very nasty, but mammon looked over at me and quickly responded. Loard is not my pet he is my most trusted friend and family and if I where you I would be incredibly careful how you speak about my future wife and your future queen. HA! HA! oh prince you are so fumy now I see why she loved you so much. Your father would never let you marry a mere human soul their beneath you. Very well you could have your pet and toy enter, I do not want you to make a fuss, but you will pay for the cleaning. I will have my people send your people my bill, this prick is really working my nerves. Yvi walked over to me and touched my shoulder, whatever I whispered to her, I looked over at Loard who was so calm and collected It did not affect him at all. We all started to walk to the main hall and Yvi said do not let him fool you. Loard is ready to kill that guy but he is calculating the correct time, not showing it his trump card. Nice like playing poker, we entered the main hall and there was a table with a feast on it. There was cake, roasted chicken corn on the cob, mash potatoes and so much more. Okay everyone sits, oh Loard He, he you must hear that a lot seeing you are the pet. That is, it I could not hold it. Listen! Here you F*** being mean and nasty is going to get you are a** Little mis please do not it is fine. Loard looked at me and showed nothing, he is a great poker player. Why your little nasty human, how dare you speak to me like that. I am royalty down here; I blame it on you prince giving false hopes as she would be more than just a nasty rude human. You always did have a soft spot for the weak, it is a shame really. I could see deep down you are very evil trying to fight it way out. ENOUGH! Mammon yelled. I swear the room shook, oh my, well I must have struck a nerve huh prince, very well let us sit everyone and enjoy while I finish getting ready. Pet and toy, I will let you eat at the table this one time for the prince sake., but this will never happen again. Prince and princess please sit on either side of the head chair. I will be down to join you shortly.

We all sat down, and I quickly started to speak but mammon cut me off and said you will sit and behave yourself as a proper future royal wife. I will not say that again, now sit and stay quiet. Now that just pissed me off, Yvi grabbed my hand looked at me in the eyes and said please sit down. What is going on here? I really do not like this game; everyone eat and enjoy our host graciously had this prepared for us so let us eat as proper royals. Mammon said as a matter of fact with grate royal influence and authority. Okay did I miss the memo, this better be all a plan because he is really pissing me off, but what I did was what he said playing along. I looked at the food and felt hungry. Okay how am I hungry, should I eat it like I normally do, I grabbed some potatoes and placed it on my plate. I stared at it for a little hoping something will magically tell me or show me what to do, so I did what any normal human does and eat. Would not you know it tasted good and I started to feel less hungry. We were all in the middle of eating when this skinny, lengthy, horrifying demon came into the room. We all stopped and stared, Mammon spoke and who might you be? I, the creature began to speak his voice was raspy and then, I am of no importance, just keep on eating the master will be down shortly he apologizes to the prince and princess for the hold up. The demon turned around and left, that was odd I told myself. Oh no he did not I think he was taking another jab at me and Loard. I ca does not stand this guy, I looked over at Mammon who was staring into his plate way to hard, but he would not even look my way. I leaned over and whispered to Yvi what is going on? Why won't he look at me? Just play your role, Yvi said. That was the only thing she said, descriptive much. Then as I was going to say something else to Yvi, this guy comes into the room. He was exceptionally good looking to, he had fire red hair, Ocean blue eyes and skin of ivory. He was dressed to the T, very fancy, Mammon quickly got up from his seat, he looked terribly upset.

What are you doing here? The guy smiled, oh my that was a beautiful smile. He was particularly good looking, oh cousin, you thought that only you could live the glory of royalty. Please, my father Michael the great arc angel and the right hand of god. I am royalty myself, once he spoke, I knew exactly who he was. The tone was so hateful, how can he be a gate keeper, aww there she is, he looked over my way and I noticed him staring at Yvi. I turned to look at her and she looked terrified, what is going on? I told myself. Oh, my Yvi do you not recognized your future husband. What? I accidently said outload, he gave me this ugly glare and hid eyes changed to the color of his hair. Oh yeah, they are defiantly related, he calmed down and said, well you are not bad looking at all for a human. I see why dear old cousin cannot get enough of you. Mammon quickly spoke out what do you want Enosi. Enosi? That is a very enchanting name I thought. Oh, little cousin sits down, the fun is about to begin I am waiting for the main attraction to arrive. Ha! Ha! He laughed and it chilled me to the core.

Chapter Ten

We were all sitting at the table just staring at each other and Enois was of course sitting at the head of the table with the most devilish smile. Well this has gotten awkward very quickly please people let speak as we wait for them to arrive. Huh, he said them that I found remarkably interesting I wonder who "Them" are. So, cousin how has it been on top with the humans? He had the most disgusted look on his face after he said "humans". I could not help myself and I spoke out, oh I see some human crushed you and now you cannot stand us, I am sorry but once a dick always a dick either here or up on earth. Watch it human, the only reason I let you on my table is for my cousin the future king. Besides, his tone changes as if he were nice, my cousin always had a soft spot for his toys and unfortunately his pets. He gave Loard a look of disgust. STOP! Looking at him like that. I said with my fist curled up. I had enough of you, want to be privileged ass. Mammon are you really going to sit there and let him disrespect us that way. Cousin Please control your toy, she is starting to irritate me and we all how I get when I am irritated. You know, come to think of it your pet is behaving better that your toy, shameful. Yvi spoke out, my future husband she smiled at him and his whole demeanor changed. So, you accept me as one of your suitors, well of course cousin to be honest cousin is there really any other that can compete with you. See I knew you would see it my way one day. The line must stay pure between the heavens and demons, mixing it with lower entities is disgusting. Did that just literally come out of his mouth, I was in shock. How can someone be so shallow? Nasty ass, he is defiantly on my shit list. Now future king you… we all hear a BOOM, BOOM, BOOM coming from the front hall. Everyone got silence as we watched his demon walk across to go answer the door. uuu, my guest has arrived, this is going to be fun, I could hear my heart beating, which the irony is that I am not supposed to have a heart let alone a heartbeat. I was feeling a little anxious, I heard the footsteps getting closer as our mystery guest makes their appearance.

There he was those eyes. Hello everyone, I hope I did not keep you waiting too long. His voice that sweet seductive voice, I felt myself just drifting. It is you I said out loud, how dare you speak to my uncle the king of hell, you disgust human. Enois, he said, and the room shook is that anyway to speak to your guests. Oh, uncle she is to my guest, I would never associate myself with her kind.She is your sons' toy, hmm he said, he began to walk over to where Mammon and Enois was at. He by passed Mammon and went straight to Enois and said do not ever disrespect my son. He walked away from Enois, who looked like he shits his pants, but there was something about his walk almost as if he was floating and those wings is big and scary, but beautiful as it flows with him as he walked. On top of all that he smelled so good; I was lost in it. He walked all the way around the table and was right behind me close behind me. He apparently does not know boundaries; he bends down to get in my face and gently grabs my face in his hands and said Hello again Yamaries. It is you was the only thing that came out. He smiled and he had the most beautiful smile just like Mammon. Yes, it is me, he kissed my forehead and all the images of him came flowing in as if they were being suppressed. I have meet you before, I was eight years old at my grandparent's house, I was in the backyard. Oh, so you remember, no not until now, I thought my grandfather was fighting with a bee that tried to sting me, but it was you.

That is right Yamaries that is the first time you could remember me, but I knew who you where before you were born. Father Mammon said what are you talking about. Oh, my son you will now soon enough.

Now everyone shall we move to the living area and have what do you call it Yamaries coffee and cake or tea and biscuits? They are both correct I told him, he smiled again and said good. He let go of my face and started to walk away, I felt a little light head and was about to fall but Yvi grabbed me before I could fall. Oh yuck, Enois said, honey please do not touch her you will catch something. Enois! Lucifer yelled that is enough of your spoiled ways. If you utter one more derogatory remark about Yamaries or my friend Loard, he turned around looked at Enois and said with a smile, there will be hell to pay. DO. I. MAKE. MYSELF. CLEAR? Enois, was terrified yes uncle as you wish. Good now have your servants fetch coffee and cake and Enois do hurry nephew I really do not like to be kept waiting. Yes, uncle right away, Enois ran out of there and was all over the place. Yvi, Mammon, Loard and sweet Yamaries follow me to the living area. As we all moved from one area to another, a lot memorize began to flash. How is this happening, I seen him more than one occasion. He has been in my life it seems like forever. We were in the living area and I was in deep thought about all my memories that I did not notice that Lucifer was on the side of me. That is right I have been there, well since the beginning of your family tree. His voice now sounding so familiar and his smell, it was overwhelmingly familiar. Go on have a seat he said we all need to talk. Enois comes in and says uncle everything is on its way, good Enois now come and sit, he quickly sat right next to Yvi who rolled her eyes in annoyance. I am glad we are all here he began, it is no mistake that we are here. No, I had nothing to do with you making it this far it was for told this way. As much as I wanted to interfere I could not, your family Yamaries was always destiny to help god in this war between demon and angels on earth. See our war should never interfere with the living ever. In the beginning yes, I killed off most of your family, it infuriated me to know that a merrier human could feel and have my father divinity. Why? Why where a human be better than us his angels that he kept in heaven with him. I did not hate all humans just your family, please do not get me wrong he did touch each human with his love, but your family got some of his divinity and was able to pass it down for generations. For that I was shun down with the demons, so I made that my soul mission to find out what about your family made you different and worthy to hold my father's divinity. As you know life goes on and I stopped hunting your family, things should I say started to get boring and your family where showing signs that the divinity might be fading. No longer a threat I decided to start my own family, now please do not mistake what I am trying to say. I stopped hunting your family, but I always kept an eye on them. When your grandfather was born everything changed. See your grandfather was supposed to be an angel but was accidently sent down to earth to become human. Lucifer laughed and that was weird his laugh was more of a shock wave than a laugh, we felt the whole room shake. Funny he continued everyone says my father does not make mistakes, turns out I am the only one who was laughing.

Enois, huffed as if he was bored, now Enois am I boring you nephew? Uncle you should not explain yourself to anyone you are king and so you never have to give reason for your actions. Oh, really Enois, funny how would you know about being a king? Uncle really? Are you serious? He looked so baffled it was hilarious. My father is Michael the right hand of god, my grandfather. Huh, I am according to stories, folklore if you like the worst of the angel's the devil, evil in carnet yet my son was taught that everything deserves reasoning. Nephew what did dear old brother teach you?How to be an insufferable pain. Now sit there and try to control yourself before I show you how to get controlled. Enois swallowed hard and said yes uncle, good now let see, ahh yes…as he continued his story, I grew more and more intrigued, our family was meant to be intertwined. Then you were born Yamaries, he continued, I was so enraged because I was not able to stop you from being born, I taught you were going to be the destruction of my family. I felt my father went too far so, on a cold night you were a month old Yamaries I snuck in to your room pulled out my knife and was going to kill you but what happened next refrained me from doing so, instead of you crying and screaming you smiled at me and surprisingly wanted me to hold you. It was quite cute, your little hands reaching out with no tears just pure love, I have never seen anything like it. I picked you up and you hugged me, and I was granted a quick glance into the future. This child was not born to destroy me or my family but to bring peace and love between the families, she was special indeed. So, for years I watched over you until my son decided to misbehave.

Mammon rolled his eyes, see Yamaries we never grow old, so I look as old as Mammon, but I am incredibly old and so is my son the prince. I smiled and said yes, I aware of the age gap, but love has no sense of time, he smiled see special.

Neither of us noticed when Enois got up and left, but he was gone. I do not think he is fawn of happy endings or that his uncle is a softy. I looked around and said umm guys where is Enois? Oh, he is right on time, he is betraying us, as you all know we are in the gate of betrayal and everyone here betrayed each other in one way or another, everyone except one. Mammon you betrayed me when you let your position of next in thrown, Yvi betrayed Mammon by not telling your brother that I was gone and Loard you betrayed Yvi by hunting down Mammon and bring him back to rule. Now Enois is betraying us all, so I ask how is it that you miss Yamaries always seems to stay so truthful to your words. Just lucky I guess, I told him, should we go looking for him? No, he will come to us. My nephew never grew up with Michael his father, I am sure he does not know what he looks like. My brother had his little excitement of being a rebel, but it was not for him. Enois was raised by his mother who is a very hateful women demon. Let us just say the boy is more demon than angel. So, what shall we talk about next Lucifer said, with so much enthusiasm? I think. He was so different than what I expected all these stories he is nothing like that, but more like a human in a way. Father why are you here telling us all of this? Mammon still sounded upset to see him. Because son, lucifer said you are going to need my help, whether you like it or not. This battle is far more than just your childish missions. It is time to think like a man and stop thinking like a child. Mammon gave his father a look that I remember all so clearly. His eyes where red and his hands where curled up into a fist. How big is this battle? I asked quickly before things got escalated. My sweet Yamaries, he said this is not just a battle my dear this is a war. The angels are coming and when they do things are not going to end well, and that brings me to you. You are the key to end this battle between my brothers and my people. You know Lucifer that I will do my best but I do not think I could get them to see reasoning, of course you are not going to change everything in one night, Lucifer said, it will take time but you will stop a fight. My brothers and I will never see eye to eye, but we will come to an understanding. Quite frankly I am okay with that he said all of this with so much confidence in me. Believe it or not sweet Yamaries but you and my son are destiny to be together, you were born to be the peace between worlds and the wife of a powerful king, my son.

The ground began to shake, oh fun has arrived but not to worry this is just the beginning. I am glad he is all happy about it, maybe he should share on his plan so we could all have the same confidence. Lucifer, I said a little quitter I did not want everyone to hear, do you really think we will get through this. He smiled and said, well my sweet it really is up to you, but I know without a doubt we will. That gave me a little bit of reinsurance, because honestly, I thought I was going to be a lost soul down here. Mammon walked over to me and hugged me, I know I have not been the best down here and I have not really been myself, but I want to let you know that I know we are meant to be. Not because my father says but because I feel it, I knew the minute I saw you, as you walked through your grandparent's door. I looked at him and said you are right you have not been yourself I think to be honest I really do not know who you are. Maybe this person who showed me down here is you. I know we are meant to be, but I am not sure you are ready for us to be. It looked a little like you are still hung up with miss thang. I am… I cut him off, that is okay first loves are hard to forget especially is she was your fiancé. Right now, at this moment everything is clear for me and that stuff is not important. Right now, the floor shook again, this is what matters I gave him a kiss and walked over to Yvi and Loard. I left him to speak with his dad and get over all his issues. You know what son, Lucifer spoke out as he watched his son's expression, she is not good one, she is a special and great one. Dad, I am not in the mood to hear your input. Yes, I know but do you think I am wrong? Of course not, I love her, I want to marry her. Good do not let those feeling go, for she will lead you down the right path. I know you are a little blinded since you got back home. These trails each gate had you find on your own and are always the hardest to fight but you are strong Mammon you will make the choice that is right, not for me or her but for yourself. Mammon faced his father Lucifer smiled and said, I might influence you to lean a little my way though. Can you believe Mammon smiled at his father and said you really are stubborn old man? Hey Lucifer, said so are you son, they both laughed together, and they sounded so majestic and hypnotizing and extremely sweet on the ears. It is nice to see dad and my brother smiling with each other again, Yvi spoke out. She looked at me and said you know dad was not okay when he left, it broke him. I guess my brother needed this to grow up. I am starting to believe my dad and what he said about you, you are here to change our worlds and I am okay with that. I smiled and told her; you know Yvi we have not be the best to one another, but I would not choice anyone else to fight alongside. That is including Loard. She smiled and said me too, Loard laughed and said little mis you are stronger than you believe and tonight you will show us how strong you really are. I was going to respond to Loard but was distracted when the sound of trumpets filled the room. Alright kids that is our sign to get up and move. Umm, move where? I asked. That my dear Lucifer said is a good question but we have to move because those are my dear brothers and they are ready, once they are here they will not leave until given a good reason to, shall we go say hello, Lucifer smiled and it was quite devilish.

We all got up and walked to the front door, I thought to myself I guess it is now or never. Lucifer smiled and opened the door; I could not believe what I was seeing we were back on earth at the house where the oldest portal is at. I did not want to lose focus, but I was a little upset, because we made it so far down there and I was so close to getting my grandfather, now I must start all over again. We walked out and the trumpets played again, this time the sky opened, and a bright light shined through. It was so magical to watch and from the light came the angels. Angels where breath taking, their wings where white, white as snow and it had gold shimmer. I looked over at Lucifer what do we do? No dear not we, you. This is your time to shine, only you could change their minds. Well shit, he was no help at all, Okay I will go., NO! Mammon said you are not going alone. She must do this alone Lucifer told Mammon. No father she does not because we never do anything alone. As someone who I love told me, we are stronger together. Let us go face them together, we began to walk towards the angels and the ground began to shake, Mammon what is going on? I have no idea, as the ground shook trees were beginning to fall, but I noticed something strange. The Angles where not moving, Mammon there is something off about those angles I yelled at Mammon trying to overpower the sound of the ground shaking and trees falling. I have noticed as well, maybe we should turn back into the house, I told him. He grabbed my hand and we began running towards the house, every time we felt like we were getting closer to the house that the house would get father away from us. Ugh! You too are boring came a voice, Enois? Is that you? Yes and no, my name is not Enois it Eminos and I am the gatekeeper of the betrayal. Prince Mammon getting you to truly betray little miss perfect is harder than I thought, I blinked and noticed we were back inside the house sitting in the living room on chairs all of us except Lucifer. What happened? I asked. Well sweetheart you are one hard cookie to break, you truly are angelic. You will never betray your little prince, what hold does he have on you? Huh? I said what are you talking about? Oh, so you really are oblivious let me tell you this little devil favorite what if I told you that he still has feelings for little miss Thang as you call her. The voice stopped talking like it was waiting for me to answer. Oh, you are asking me a question? Do not play dumb with me, we both know that you do not like her. I was insecure about it at first but now I am not, it is his choice and he alone must make it. Suddenly this figure comes out from behind the wall and says I am very intrigued. You are rare, this gate keeper looked like a normal human, he had brown hair, brown eyes, and a Carmel color skin. You are a gate keeper? Everyone else looked different, well, well are not we are being a little judge. Do all your people look alike? We demon gods all look different. Did everything that happen was a lie? Well he said yes, and no. Explain please I told him. Well the whole angels already begin here is a lie, I am quite sure you sort of knew that but everything else is true. Did I meet Lucifer? That part is true he got into my muse, Tricky, tricky King but he did make it interesting and easy for me to follow and to play it all in my plan. Now you, he sounded a little creepy when he said that Yamaries I would like to ask you something. Umm, okay what is it? Mammon tilted his head a little I guess it was to hear better. You know I have been living down here for a millennium and I never thought I would see a day where I would find someone that is worthy enough for me. Oh My god, is he going to ask me, Yamaries would you marry me and just like that there was a box with a ring in his hand. Mammon's eyes got bright red, he stared at Eminos, how dare you he finally said. Yvi quickly tried to intervene, brother do not. Who are you to try and rip us apart, mammon roared? Oh, Little Prince you are still hooked on Zora, why do you care if she marries me, you will have Zora. Selfish little Prince you want them both. Well sorry prince this rooster seen this hen and he wants. She is not a toy! He yelled and it make the room shake. Oh no Prince I would never, Yamaries you are no a toy, I want you to be my wife. I would never ask a toy to be mine in that way. You will never have her Mammon said. Hello, I am still here, I could answer for myself and you I turned to him why are you so upset is not that what you tried to hide from me. Yamaries I never… Stop, it takes someone else to want me for you to get scared and you, you do not even know me. How can you ask me to marry you, I was not always this way, I was a horrible person a couple of years back? I am not who you think I am. Mm, that is right and that is what fascinates me. Yuck, I said to myself. Stop, both of you stop, Eminos we need to get to the last gate, obviously no one here is going to betray one another, our bond is big. Hmm, you might be right, for now but why do not I make you a deal say you will marry me, and I will let you go to the next gate. No, I will say yes if we all get to leave including you. Yvi spoke out no Yamaries do not do this, Little mis please. Loard plead, mammon said nothing just stared. Brother stop her, do not let her do this. She could do as she wished, mammon said. Little mis he does not mean that it does not matter, my deal stands.Oh, Yamaries you will do this to help everyone else, no I said, I will do this to save my grandfather and stop a war that should never begin. So selfless, yes you will be a great wife, I Eminos the gatekeeper of betrayal humbly… Stop! Mammon yelled you will let us go to the next gate without Yamaries. Oh, he, he prince please enlighten me. That made it worse, no I said do not intervened a deal is a deal.I will need for you Loard and Yvi to trust me, he looked at me and said I cannot, I am not going to lose you. No, Eminos you are going to make a deal with me because if you do not, I will make sure you will no longer be the keeper of this gate. Oh, and if you think I cannot, let us go ahead and test this theory out. Oh, well prince now I see why sweet Yamaries feel so hard for you, I guess what human say are correct opposites do attract. Well Prince since, we all know you do have that power now that you and daddy are buddies again. What deal would you like to make, oh, and prince do not be shy with it. He smiled and it creeped me out, if you take us directly to gate eight, I would introduce you to Zora, and he said you could join us in this little adventure through gate eight. Hmm, very tempting prince but I do not want Zora, I want Yamaries, she is the one for me and prince she would never have eyes for anyone but you. So, prince, we are back to Yamaries deal it sounds fun. I gave Mammon a look that says trust me, he gave me a small bow in approval. Okay then Eminos we shall complete the deal. I Eminos accept the deal that was bestowed upon me by Yamaries. This green light almost as if a tiny firefly rapped itself around my arms. These lights gave me a tattoo looking vine that rapped around my arm up to my elbow. What is this? Well my soon to be bride this is like an engagement ring. Oh okay, I said it is pretty, he came closer to me and grabbed my hand, he looked in my eyes and kissed my cheek.

You are incredibly beautiful, and I am glad you like it, when we get finished with our mission, we could get married. Would you prefer a big wedding? We could even invite the prince; this could help you prince with ideas for yours with Zora. My heart broke when he said that, and my light green tattoo turned red and burned. Ouch, oh its burning, Mammon, Yvi and Loard came rushing over. Mammon quickly roared, what are you doing to her? Oh, Prince you did not think that it would not come with a price. She will learn to love me and forget you, one way or another. Every time she thinks about you the tattoo as she calls it will change color informing me and begin to burn. See my sweet you will forget Mammon because thinking about him will hurt a lot. Mammon's eyes got red and he was ready to pounce on him, but Loard grabbed his arm and said master do not we need to press on. The burning began to subside, and I looked at Eminos and said we are going to need to trust each other, so I apologize for this, can we please leave? I am so glad I made you my wife so sweet, yes, we do need to trust each other but as you could see I cannot right now. Now let us press on to gate eight, this may take a little because I cannot just make portals like everyone else, see no one ever made it this far so no need to learn. I guess I am just special I said and grabbed his hand and smiled at him. He smiled back and said yes you are, okay everyone this way. We walked over to the kitchen and out the back door. We began walking through the woods and I cannot believe how hot it was and steamy. It felt like we were walking for hours, can we please take a break I feel like I am going to pass out. Oh, my sweet we sure can, it must be hard carrying the weight of the soul's fault's. excuse me? Oh, this forest, it is the forest of soul's faults. So only the purest carries the faults and my beautiful bride to be you are defiantly are the purest. He turned to Mammon and said are not I the luckiest demon alive. Mammon murmured something as he walked away. Loard looked at Eminos and said you are hurting your bride to be. What are you talking about? She is not in pain only tired. Oh, really Loard said is it me or is anyone else seeing the black spot growing on the side of her neck. Mammon quickly walked over to me touched me and all I could remember was how he use to touch me before we started this little adventure. I could not help it and my tattoo began to burn, OUCH! I said, Eminos walked over to Mammon and said stop touching her, now look who is hurting her he said to Loard. My love let me look at your spot, Oh, my I did not know this was going to happen, I heard about it only I have not really seen it. See some of these faults are not genuinely nice if you get my drift. Some faults are awfully bad and could stain the pure crushing them and turning the purest of soul's dark. What? Eminos you never said anything about this. Sorry my love but I never thought you were that pure. Excuse me? What? Oh, like you all did not think that, well this is a problem we must move and get her some help. Okay smart ass Yvi said where are we going to find her help, no one else is here besides us. Maybe getting her to the other gate I guess, I do not know everything. Apparently not, brother what do you think? I have no idea Yvi, but he might be right as painful as it is for me to admit. Yamaries Mammon said are you able to move? Yes, I could keep going, I got up and I began walking towards the path. I bumped into Eminos and pushed him out of the way, Yvi followed me Yamaries? Yes Yvi, I am sorry for all of this, I know we started off very rough, but no one deserves all this. I really do hope we could become friends, she made me laugh Yvi we are friends, no we are more than friends we are family. She smiled and said I like that; I hope we get to that gate soon Yvi between you and me I am not sure how long I could hold on.

What do you mean? I showed her my shoulder that was already black. Yamaries why did not you say something before, I am just trying to get to gate eight and get my grandfather and get out of this mess. You know it is hard to get of this magic, Yvi said. Yeah but we have a trump card, your dad. I have a feeling he might know a trick or two, she smiled you are one of a kind. Yeah, I know we both laughed, Eminos came up to us and said ladies, you are going the wrong way, I did not know if you knew that. Yvi its over there to the left you will find your brother and that thing. We just looked at him, chop, chop Yvi I need to talk to my future wife. Yvi rolled her eyes and walked off, Eminos I said his name is Loard, I sounded as if I was having a hard time breathing. What? He replied, I said his name is Loard, not thing. Do not you ever say that again, oh my sweet you have the most beautiful heart. Do you want me to buy him for you? I see you have grown attached to it and I do not want to take it away. I grabbed him by his shirt and said I will F*** you up if you keep talking about him like that, do I make myself clear? Oh, my sweet Yamaries please calm down I do apologize I did not mean to offend my beautiful fiancé. He... Is... Not... For... Sale, I let go of him and pushed him away. Umm, Yamaries we are not done, Oh Eminos yes, we are. I walked to where Yvi and Mammon where at and I grabbed Loard and gave him a big hug. Little mis are everything okay? Yes, I just want to let you know that I will not let anyone disrespect you. Loard laughed and said I know little mis, I know. Mammon walked over to me and said, "we are close" Mammon said, "how do you know?" I said, "I could feel the darkness", mammon said. I do not think I am going to make it, "what do you mean?" he sounded concerned. I was starting to feel dizzy and I started to stumble, Mammon catches me funny the tattoo did not burn, I looked up at Mammon and said thank you. Yamaries! Eminos said as he is running towards Mammon. Give her to me, he said as if he was there the whole time. This is your fault if she turns, I will see you die. Calm down prince look over there, it is the gate. We just got to go through it, Eminos rubbed my face and said with such a sweet voice, we are here my love you are going to get better. Please I do not feel good, please I begged. The pain I was feeling was horrible it was almost as bad as when Mammon and I merged for the first time. Eminos looked at Mammon we need to hurry, she dies Mammon said so will you. Stop being so dramatic prince she is not going to die; she will just turn bad that is all. She will nor let that happen she would rather die first, and you know it that is why you are trying to rush us. Do you not know how to talk and move prince? We need to move now Eminos said, brother we must move. Fine Mammon said he went to go grab me but Eminos was not having it, DO not touch her! I will be carrying my fiancé there. No! you need to open that gate. I can not only she can and you... Enough! Both of you, we must move, look, Yvi said. I had black blushes covering the side of my face, Mammon who was half holding on to me, completely rip me out of Eminos arms and ran, he ran right in front of this big black gate that had purple ominous light around it. Mammon I said, I love you and I will wait for you until the end of time. Everything went dark, I am not sure what happened or how we got inside but we did, and I started to regain consciousness.

Hello Yamaries, a woman's voice said, I really could not see who it was, it was blurry, but I answered back. Hello, are you the keeper of gate eight? She laughed it was so soft and pretty. I blinked and rubbed my eyes to try and focus, and when my vision straightens out there was this demon not scary, she was beautiful for a demon that is. She had long black hair, purple eyes, black horns, and very pale skin. Well Yamaries my name is Luna, I am Yvi's and Mammon's mom. Oh, nice to meet you, aww I see the rumors are true you are extremely sweet. What happened? Eminos right away answered, you lost consciousness my love but do not worry I took care of you and look you are healing perfectly. Do not lie to her Luna said you were not so concern over her, you where more concern over my son touching her. Yeah, I told her that sounds about right. Are you able to get up? Yeah, I am just a little tired I guess from fighting this thing. That is correct you are stronger than you look. I stood up and felt kind of dizzy but did not really show it. I finally started looking around at my surrounding and noticed that the sky was purple and the grass and trees where black. I touched the bush that was next to me to see if it was dead or rotten. Would you believe it, the leaf's were alive, I was impressed, I am not going to lie everything flowed so beautifully, can you believe it looks like the leaves where being blown by the wind but I could not feel the wind. I see what my son sees in you, Luna startled me a little. Everything you see is amazing to you, he says that he loves looking at you when he shows you something. He says you are always so intrigued; He also says he loves all the facial expressions you make with your emotions. All I could say was, oh he did? You know this is not something any guy would say or look at, but my son always been a softy for true love. Yeah, I have heard, but right now he has a lot of thinking to do. She smiled, and it was beautiful, well you will be surprised on how much thinking he has done. I changed the conversation because this was starting to get weird. So, who is the gate keeper of gate eight? Yes, gate eight the gate of darkness, well sweet girl that would be me Luna Morning star.

Chapter Eleven

was in shock, you? How did that happen? Oh, my dear this was my choice. I always wanted my own world in my own image. Lucifer gave me this gate so I could build and mold it into my image and I love him for it. Umm I thought... I stopped mid-sentence, but she finished it for me. That you are supposed to be some way true to the gate, mean, malicious? I am sorry I did not ... oh, stop, she said I know, I could feel that you would never, she smiled. See some demons are only plain evil and love to torture, I was never like that and will never be. Well I guess I might be a little bad, I left my children with Lucifer without telling them goodbye. I guess I am evil, you know I never really said that out loud before. My kids should hate me, but they do not, they love me just the same. I smiled and said I think their dad did a good job in letting them know how much you love them, maybe she said with a smile, maybe. Do you get many souls visitor's here? She laughed, no, they barely make it out of gate one. I did hear about you and your friends and I had to see for myself, but I did hear the prince of hell was with you so I could not stop at the opportunity to see my son and a bonus to see my daughter as well. I smiled and looked over at Mammon and Yvi they looked happy, which is rare for them. So, you are looking for your grandfather... she looked at me like I should finish the sentence. Soul, I said, yes, we heard he was here, but I think it might have been a mistake. Oh, why would they think it would be here? I know I am not sure, but we have been through a lot for nothing it looks like. Well you guys do not have to leave right away, why do not you come to my place and get some rest before you go back home. Mom, Mammon said, is there a way maybe you could help us secretly of course find Zozo? I could see what I could do come follow me. Let me get you guys indoors and settled in, you guys look a mess. I smiled that sounds like a great plan, thank you. We walked through the forest and seen these animals that where luminousness, it looked just like a frog except in purple, a glowing purple. I quickly realized that all the animals where glowing. This gate should not be this beautiful I said softly to myself. It is beautiful like you, a voice came from the side of me. I stood calm because I still had tattoos, thank you I said and my tattoo started to burn, but it was not so bad. Oh, Yamaries I am sorry I forgot to Mammon said, that is okay, honestly, I forgot to. He smiled you know I never thought I would see my mother ever again and it took meeting you to reunite us. I looked at him, no Mammon you found her because this was the path you choose. You were always meant to find your mom, this time you tried a little harder. We were in deep conversation and did not realize that we made it to Luna's house. She lived on a beautiful mansion, of course the house was black, she had picture size windows with blue curtains not just any blue but fluorescent blue at that. She loves fluorescent colors. We walked in and her house had the same layout as Lucifer's home. She walked over to Mammon and I said I always loved this home; I just gave it a twist she smiled and walked off. She is right, she loved our home and made sure everything was perfect for dad. Her home was black and blue in the inside it was just as beautiful as the black and red. She turned to all of us and said make yourselves at home, Loard, Yvi and Mammon I am quite sure you know your way around. Please ask them Eminos and Yamaries to take you wherever you need. Oh, umm, Yamaries your room is meant for you and my son, Eminos you will sleep in the other guest room. I did not know you where coming. Yvi and Loard you know your rooms. Go freshen up and we will meet at the dinner table, enjoy my home. Umm, Luna? Eminos said Yamaries is my fiancé as you see from the tattoo. Luna did not look impressed, oh yes that pesky little thing. Yamaries sweetheart hold up your arm, Luna brought up her hands and said "Endecto Reversento" and this purple light came down rapped itself around the tattoo and poof the tattoo was gone. Eminos, I will tell you this, one I am older so your little childish spells are nothing and two you should never force a woman to be with you by force it is disgusting and rude even for a demon level. Now go and try not to annoy me, she is awesome I turned to Mammon and said I love your mom. He smiled and said so do I. Yvi ran over to us and gave me a hug, I am so glad you do not have to marry stinky over there. Me too, I told her with a lot of excitement in my voice. Mammon looked over at me and said shall we go get ready for dinner. I felt myself get all heated up I am quite sure my face was red. Yvi looked at her brother and said I will meet you both back at the dinning room. Loard passed by us and said master, little mis bowed his head and walked down the hall. Eminos looked over at us and said this is not over, he walked away and went down the hall as well. Mammon grabbed my hand and said well our sweet is up there, okay I said and grabbed his hand back. It felt good to have him hold my hand like this again. We walked up the stairs and down the hall and would you know it the room is the last one by the picture window. This is starting to get creepy, we walked in and the room is something out of the movies, the walls were of course black, the carpet was royal blue, the bed was old fashion canopy in black with royal blue sheets. There was also a big fireplace and would you know there is a balcony and a double opened door. I could not feel the wind blowing before but up here on the balcony the minute I opened the doors the beautiful breeze flowed through my hair. I took a deep breath and could smell the beautiful changes of the leaves and a light touch f cold; I love autumn. I felt arms come from behind me and hold me. It felt good I had to admit, I love the of being in gulfed in his arms. He laid his head on top of mine and took a deep breath and said you always smell so perfect. I turned around and held him, now we were face to face and I said I thought we were never going to hold each other like this again. He said I thought I was going to loose you forever, but before something like that happens again Mammon said Yamaries he got down on one knee and said would you do me the honor of being Mrs. Morning star. I started to cry and said yes, I smiled. He smiled and kissed me, He waved his hand and just like that, this beautiful black and red ring came out of this air. The diamond was red and big the band was black shiny with small red diamonds around it. It was a little flashy, but I was not complaining the ring is beautiful, I told him. He looked at me and said this Journey through these gates had me so confused but once I thought I lost you that is what made me realize that I am deeply and deathly in love with you. I cannot live without you; I know that no matter what you will always be there for me and my family. I smiled and told him I know that you are my forever. I see you always as the man that holds me up and empowers me. Well needles to say that in that moment I became a woman, so my grandmother would say. We where both in bed and realized we needed to hurry up and get ready for dinner, we quickly showered and got ourselves together and went downstairs.

Everyone was already at the dinner table and Luna looked at us smiled and said I am glad you two can join us. I am so, so, sorry I told her, no need dear just have a seat, we walked over to the seats nest to her. Oh, my dear your engagement ring is beautiful, Yvi looked over quickly and said let me see. I placed my hand on the table so everyone could see, Congratulations Yvi said I am finally going to have a sister to talk to. I smiled, welcome to the family little mis Loard said. Eminos looked terribly upset, Luna said yes dear welcome and your glowing as well is someone a woman now. My smiled left my face, I felt like she was being a little malicious by saying that in front of Eminos. Umm, that is private please, I said. Oh, my dear of course, she clapped her hands and the servants started bringing the food out. I looked at them and said to myself where did they come from. I swear I did not see them before, I brushed it off because the food smelled so good it was steak and potatoes my favorite. They served wine and water, Luna got up and clanged her glass and said this has turned into a night of me seeing my children in a longtime to an engagement celebration and I am proud mom. My son you could not have picked a more perfect girl for yourself, long… she was interrupted by a loud boom, everything happened so fast after that. These demons came rushing in at first I did not realize who the demons where and like a ton of bricks a light went off, they are want to be demons, where is Mammon I have to tell him, before I could find Mammon one them grabbed me from behind and blew this powder in my face and said "Sono Uminos" and everything went black.

I awoke and noticed the noragar in front of me, I pushed back a little and noticed I was bound to a chair and I could not speak. My, my Yamaries how the tables have turned for you. That voice, I hate that voice, I looked down to see if I could unravel the ropes that where holding me down, so I thought. Instead I was in the middle of a pentagram, I was bound by a spell, not roped, I am always thinking like a human, if I keep making these mistakes I will lose. I looked up and around, I noticed Mammon is hanging with his hands up and legs bounded together and he is also in the middle of a pentagram but it was a little different he had some writing or symbols that looks like no one has ever seen. Ha, ha, oh Yamaries you could look around, but you will never get out. I have been waiting for you, you the one who fought me and lived to tell the tale. Now when I heard you were looking for me, I felt honored, I was not going to let you look so long but then I heard dear old prince was joining you. Why would I think he would not, he loves his human? I knew things where going to get complicated, so I gave the little informant some false information that the dumb servant wanted to hear. Loard has never been very smart. I tried to say something, but I could not, oh Zozo said no, no I bounded your mouth with a spell I do not want to hear you, your voice annoys me. I looked around and noticed we were still in Luna's house but no sign of Luna. Something awful must of happened to her, Mammon and Yvi is going to be devastated. I kept looking around frantically I need to figure something, anything. Oh Yamaries are you looking for me, would you like to know what I look like I am pretty sure you are dying to know, oh look at that Ha, I just made myself laugh, you are already dead. I feel particularly important for you to kill yourself to find me, thank you I am honored.

So, because of this I will grant you that, to have the privileged to lay eyes on pure evil and greatness. He came out from the darkness right in front of me, he was something different all together at first glance he looked human but there is emptiness in those eyes, his teeth are pointy, black eyes pale very pale. He said take it all in Yamaries, I am perfection. Well almost once I get angel let just say essence, I will be unstoppable. I will be god's number one assassin, he stood straight up with his hand in the air as if embracing himself. I thought to myself wow this demon is very arrogant, he will never be thought of as a good enough to become gods number one, because god is just not like that. He kept talking and that annoyed me, why is he still talking he can not be that into himself. In the middle of his dialog my vision began to get blurry, I shook my head a little bit to try and focus my vision but instead it got worse I started getting dizzy and I finally passed out. When I came to, I was in a big room realizing right away I was in Lucifer's den. I looked around and noticed I was able to speak, hello? Shh, Yamaries I am going to make this quick, I am on my way with some help, I am sorry sweet Yamaries you are going to go through a lot of pain, but you are a strong girl and you will be okay. Lucifer what is going on? How did this happen? Shh, Yamaries just know that help is on its way, and please try to keep my son alive. I promise I will, I manage to say and Yamaries he said welcome to the family. He smiled and everything went black again. When I cam e to Zozo was in my face how dare you fall asleep while I am talking, what do I bore you? Let me tell you a little secret honey this is no ordinary pentagram you are in, it is very old and it was used for torture, he shook all over once he said that. What a psychopath, the fact that he could find that amusing is sickening. Would you know it, it is your lucky day I am going to show you how it works? He walked back a little raised his hands and said oops almost forgot one of the main steps silly me, he looked over at mammon and snapped his fingers. Mammon awoke, what is going on? He said oh little prince you finally awoken just in time to; I am about to put on a show. Zozo leave her alone, oh yeah Zozo smiled this is going to be fun. He once again raised his hands and said "Exnotramos, enos, luximos" the pentagram glowed, and some invisible words appeared. I looked around in fright, what is going on? I looked at him and he was smiling. "Ominous, extrano, eus" I thought I was going to die, the pain, the burning started from my feet and it rose to my head. I began to scream, surprisingly my voice is back, I felt my blood begin to boil my head had so much pressure. I just screamed in agony, Mammon began to scream, STOP! PLEASE STOP! Zozo laughed and he sound as if he was very much enjoying this. I finally passed out, I could not take the pain any longer, I woke up and I felt like I got hit a semi-truck. I pulled up my head and noticed Zozo was not in the room, I looked over at mammon and he was all bloody. I panicked, mammon? I called out Mammon please I began to cry. MAMMON! Oh, honey stop yelling. I looked over at the doorway and Luna was there, oh Luna I am so glad to see that you are okay. How did you escape? Hurry he is not here come get us down. She just stood there staring at me and she began to laugh. Oh, sweet gullible Yamaries I am not here to let you go, no I just came to check on my son. You could die for all I care. My son needs to learn and let go of that stupid idea of loving a human and then he made it worse by asking you to marry him. Yuck, you touched my baby boy, you, and your angelic essence. He is so much like his father it is just disgusting. Why? You have Yvi, oh please Yvi is so needy always trying to make some one proud so we could love her, she is weak to be a pure demon. She might look like us, but she is no demon she is just like her dad as well. It is sad really. How can you be so mean to your children, I never wanted to get pregnant, I just wanted to be with the most powerful man in hell, I eventually did, but then I got pregnant and the kids killed everything. You where right about one thing I was sent here by Lucifer himself as punishment for trying to drown Mammon and Yvi when they where one years old. So, your thoughts where right about me, I am evil, I married Lucifer for money and power, but I am with Zozo because he is my soulmate and as you see we are both demons. My son id the future King of hell and he needs someone who is going to be the best queen and you human and angel hybrid are not. She walked over to Mammon and started to wipe his face, I am sorry my son, but you need to learn that this is not okay. She grabbed his face in her hand looked at him, ugh you look like your father. I should have finished killing you when you where young but no Zozo wanted you alive. He has plans for you, Mammon opened his eyes they where bright red and he gave her the hardest head bud I have ever heard. Luna screamed and tumbled backwards, you disrespectful little shit. She touched the area that he hit and wiped the blood and licked it, she smiled and said hmm, maybe you are more like me than I think. She turned to me and said, I hope you hold on a little longer, I want to see the pain in my dear old son's face as the light goes from your eyes. She smiled and said tout a l'heure as she walked out of the room. What a twisted chick, Mammon I said. Yamaries, my love you are alive, yes, honey I am alive I have something to live for. He smiled, you are bleeding from your nose and mouth. I am fine I promise we must get out of here. Oh, trying to leave so soon, but the party just started Zozo said. Funny you two think you have it bad, you should see what you are so call mommy is doing to your dear sister and your favorite servant. I do have to admit, I hoped she does not hurt your sister to much she is beautiful, and I might want to take her as my bride, your mom is starting to get old. Anyways let us play shall we. So, Mammon did you make my wife bleed? What did not like what mommy had to say. It is true she wanted to prove her love for me by killing you and your sister so when I kill Lucifer, I will be king, but now I see that was thinking small. Once she got caught and I did as well, she was banished here and I knew she would wait for me, see I am her only. Oh, and you think she is your only let see how much she means to you, Mammon. Leave her alone! Why? When your pain is so much better. He walked over to me and said now try to stay up longer it is no fun when you pass out early. Okay, now have patience with me I have never tried this one before. "Anubious, inferno, Maximums" my whole body jolted, it is like I got hit by a bolt of lightning. He laughed yes; I love this one how about you? STOP! Leave her alone! Your problem is with me. Oh, prince it is not always about you. "Anubious, somo, extrano" I felt like my chest collapsed and I quickly spat up blood and passed out once again.

Let this be the end, I am not sure if I could keep going, I was battling and fighting to come back and suffer some more which seems so hard, or letting go and just finish it all which seemed easier. The I remember what Lucifer said, "you are going to suffer but I know you will be okay, you are strong girl." No, I said to myself I cannot give up I have to fight, they will be coming soon. I finally woke up and I could feel pain everywhere which is off, because I am a spirit someone please explain this to me. I looked up and around and I did not see Mammon. I panicked a little, I am here all alone, oh, hello you are up again well this is disappointing I really did think you where done. You are a strong girl, so I guess Luna is going to be upset your little prince is ready to give in to dear old mommy. Maybe, I should not say anything and let the prince crack, now you Yamaries I am going to crack, Let see Zozo said Oh I know he said as if he came up with the best idea ever. I know what you want, he smiled, and I am going to give it to you. That is odd Yamaries thought, Zozo is a monster why would he give me what I want. Eggnorat, he called out bring him to me. I looked around to see what he is talking about. I was looking at Zozo because I was waiting for him to do something, but a bright light caught my attention. I tried to look behind him as if I could move, he smiled and said, our guest of honor is here and smiled. The bright light got closer, as the light reached the corner, I felt my heart skipped a beat. There he was my grandfather, in chains, looking down he walks right in eyesight, not to close to me but not far either. Hello, my little pet, because you have been such a good boy, I got you a present. It infuriated me to hear him speak to my grandfather like that, grandpa I spoke first, he quickly looked up, Yamaries is that you? Yes, grandpa it is me and I began to cry. Grandpa… well I think that is enough, No please wait I have not … you have not what pet? You are going to stop talking to him like that, or what sweet Yamaries, you are going to do what? Ha, ha, do not make me laugh, I was born from hatred and raised with hatred, your empty threats irritates me. I am going to show you what happens when you annoy me, Eggnorat take grandpa where her beloved Mammon was at. NO! oh, hush now this is going to be fun, well for me anyway, he smiled at me and I wanted to punch him. My pet because you decided to speak back to me, I am going to show you that you should never talk back to me. I knew what he was going to do. I braced myself, I just started at my grandfather, just looked in his eyes. I knew I was going to be okay when I looked at him.

I love you grandpa, I mouthed out to him, he began to cry. Zozo raised his hand and said "inferto… and he got interrupted. Who the hell thinks they could interrupt me? Oh, you are going to bring that to a two Luna said. You could talk to your pet and servants like that, but you will never speak like that to me the queen of hell. Zozo turned his head at her and said you are no longer queen of hell my dear, Lucifer left you here to rot you are nothing but a low demon crawling and scratching your way back up and please remember that without me you are nothing. This demon is the embodiment of evil, I can not believe he talks to her like that, I do not feel sorry for her for her but even I think that was to low, Luna placed her head down and said do not be nasty. She is supposed to be dead and I find you playing with your pet and your food. Did your mother does not teach you some manners, he placed this disgusted look at her and said I killed and ate my mother, and I would be careful if I where you. If I did that to my mother imagine what I would do to you. She got close to him and was faced to face and said do not push me Zozo you do not scare me. He smiled and kissed her, oh, yuck I said was that their sick way of fore play. They both make me sick. Zozo my son senses little mis thang here, he will not budge, he says, and I quote "I know she is alive because our love is strong." Ugh, it is quite disgusting. So, Luna dear what do you want me to do? Stop playing around and finish her off, you are wasting time. LUNA! Do not rush me I am the king of torture it is fun for me and I need it, if you like I could bring your son back and torture him some more. It is your choice lover. Eww, he called her lover, I think I am going to throw up. Well I guess I could let you play with him a little more, he is starting to bore me. You know Luna, you should do yourself a favor and kill your own son, it is exhilarating, there is nothing like it. Unless you are to soft to do it, stop pushing

Zozo or the one I am going to make my bitch is you. She turned around and stormed out, Zozo huffed, I hate having her around. He looks at me and said she does not understand the art of torture that is why she does not find it fun. I on the other hand am a master of my work. I sometimes empress myself, okay so where were we oh yes in the middle of torturing you. Now pay attention, he looked over at my grandfather this is going to be painful, Zozo raised his hands one more time "infernto…" Once again, he was interrupted master, we must speak. IF YOU DO NOT STOP INTERUPTING ME, I AM GOING TO LOSE IT! The servant lowered his head and said sorry master, NOW GO! Yes sire. AHHHH! He yelled they are upsetting; how can I be surrounded by idiots. I think once I am done with you, I am going to kill them all. I had just about enough, he took a deep breath and said you know what I am so irritated that I think I am going to make myself feel better. He turned looked at my grandfather and said "Inferanto unos" my grandfather screamed in pain, NO STOP! He looked as if he was going to burst from his scream. Please I pleaded, please. This broke me and all I could do is cry and tell him you broke me, please leave him alone, please. Oh, that is it Yamaries give me what I want. "Numos" he said and turned his hand to the side, my grandfather screamed. It was a blood curling scream, then there was silence, I could not look over at all I thought he was gone, he evaporated or whatever spirits do when they are vanished. I screamed NO! WHY!? How could you? I could not take this pain, I wanted it all to end and he quickly said yes, that is exactly what I was looking for. That desperation of losing and the loneliness, see he laughed my work is art, and this is my masterpiece. You are a monster! I yelled out to him, he smiled and said thank you, I do my absolute best. He began to laugh, I am so thirsty I had a long night, I am leaving now but I will be back. I will leave you here with grandpa, Tout a l'heure. He walked off laughing, I struggled to get loose all I wanted to do was kill him, I did not want to but I grabbed some guts and looked over at where my grandfather was at and he was still there, he just looked like he passed out. Grandpa? I called out to him. Grandpa, please wake up, he did not move or say anything. I lowered my head and felt hopeless, how could I have let this happen. I thought to myself. If I am the hero and suppose to save the Angel and demon world, why could I not do something as simple as saving my grandfather. Was it that? Was it because I thought it was going to be simple? My mind was going a mile per minute with no solution. I was so deep in thought that I did not hear my grandfather begin to moan, I was startled when I heard my name being called, Yamaries? I turned around quickly, Grandpa? Yamaries are you okay? Oh, grandpa I began to cry, grandpa you are okay. Did he hurt you? Grandpa he did try, but you are okay and that is more important to me. You are the world to me, grandpa we must get out of here and find Mammon. Who is Mammon? Oh, there is a lot to tell you but there is not enough time, just know that he is good and strong, and he will get us out of here. We cannot leave without him, my grandfather said we must kill him and his little minions. Yes, grandpa I know but we are going to need help. I have brought help with me, but we all got caught. Really? Who did you bring? Did you bring your grandmother and your aunt? Wow, he has jokes even in the face of danger, I smiled and said very funny grandpa you know I would never bring grandma. He laughed too and said god, I hope you did not bring your aunt. I started to laugh too, it felt good to laugh, I do not remember the last time I laughed like this. My grandfather and I where so caught up with us just being ourselves that we did not noticed that someone came in. Little mis? I heard and quickly looked at the doorway, I knew that voice. Loard! Oh, it is so good to see you, I thought something bad happened. Loard, began to walk over to me and my grandfather yelled do not get close to her. No, grandpa it is okay he is my friend. He is a demon mija, you cannot trust him. Grandpa, please hear me out, I trust Loard with my life, he has helped me through a lot during this journey and I made it to you. Loard looked surprised he smiled and turned to my grandfather and said grandpa sir, I would never do anything to hurt little mis for she is the future queen of hell. Oh shit, I said to myself why would he say that my grandfather is going to flip shit. I looked over at my grandfather, scared to hear what he was going to say, but he did not say anything just stared. How can I trust you or your kind all you have done is twist the truth to help yourselves? Grandpa he would never lie to me or to, thank god he did not believe him, I did not want to explain that right now. Loard we must move before he comes back you must get us out. Yes, little mis no time to argue, he was walking over to me, but I stopped him. No, get my grandfather first, No Yamaries you. Grandpa now is not the time, Loard walked over to him raised his hand and said "Salvento Extratos" and my grandfather fell to the floor. Grandpa, are you okay? Yes, yes, I am fine, Loard went to go help him but my grandfather pulled away and said I do not need help from you. I felt bad for Loard, grandpa do not be like that he just saved you. No little mis it is okay, here let me release you, as he was walking towards me, he said I am sorry I did not get here faster little mis. Loard you do not have to apologize I failed you, Yvi and Mammon, I am the one who should be sorry. Loard smiled, still creepy but I still felt incredibly grateful, little mis I told you royalty never apologize, but friends and family do Loard always remember that. Little mis this is going to be hard, but I think I remember these spells from master. I trust you Loard, "Amunos Enfartamos Tutormos" I felt as if ropes where beginning to loosen up and I could move a little. "sufrento No Masmo" and just like that I was free from my bind. I feel off the chair and hit the floor. It felt good to be free, come on little mis and grandpa we have to save master, Loard walked towards the door, he did not realize that he walked right into a knife that went right through him. NO! I yelled as I watched Loard fall to the ground and land in a pool of his blood. Ugh I always hated his pale, nasty, know it all ass. I have waited millenniums to kill him. It feels great, she said as she smiled over his body.

Chapter Twelve

I was in a state of shock, I did not know if I should cry, scream, or fight. How can you be so heartless? The words just slipped out of my mouth without me thinking about it. Luna smiled and said apparently you must not know me thus far, sweet Yamaries I do not have a heart to be heartless. I do recall my dear husband and my mother calling me a monster, but I would like to think of myself as ruthless. I wanted to slap that smile off her face. She started to walk closer to me and said you know what? I would do it all over again if I had the chance. He was annoying and very nosey, he had what was coming to him, I jumped at her and I never noticed when my grandfather got to me, but he held me back and said in my ear. No Yamaries do not react to crazy she will kill you on the spot. I knew he was right, but I was fuming with anger. I do not know when it started but I began to cry, my tears were just flowing. STOP! Your stupid human emotions, you humans with all your emotions just annoys me. I tried lunging at her again but once again, my grandfather held me back. Yamaries gain control of your emotions, we must be patient I have faith that we will have help soon. I was so exhausted and hurt that I just laid completely down and cried, I cried until my eyes hurt. Luna looked at me with so much disgust, she began to speak, and

I am sure it was a speech on human emotions. I could se her mouth moving but I could not hear anything that was coming out. I suddenly began to hear sounds of trumpets, but it was incredibly low, I thought at first that I might have been out of it but then the sound got louder. I quickly began to sit up and my grandfather quickly said do not react, I told you that we were getting help soon. I smiled a little and she stopped in the middle of her sentence and said have I said something to amuse you. I quickly realized that I might have made a mistake, but I played it off very well. I am smiling because I am going to kill you, it might not be right now but one day I will. She laughed and said oh I am looking forward to it. When she said that she had a twinkle in her eye as if she could envision the bloody fight, that I am not going to lie was scary to see. She snapped herself out of the daydream of our fight and said well I am over talking to you, I am going to see if my son has died already, I have to give it to him, he is a strong man. What? You would never kill your son, she smiled and said as she was walking out oh yes, I would, and you can trust me on that I am evil incarnate. She turned that corner and then I was going to say something to my grandfather and she popped right back in and said you know, you and my son are two that are very hard to break but I give up and you both need to die. I will let Zozo know, she once again turned the corner and walked out of the room. I waited a little before I said anything to my grandfather because I did not want her to know or him for that matter. I quickly turned to my grandfather once I realized she was not coming back in and said grandpa we must do something quick I di believe she will kill him. Yamaries you must believe that he could take care of himself remember he is the prince of hell and I am quite sure he knows how to handle his mother. Grandpa I know you are right, but I need to help him, NO! you need to help yourself first before you can help him. You are so focus on him that you never realized that we are not tied up and no guards are at the door, we are able to run out. He was right they have forgotten we were untied and are able to move around the castle, grandpa you are right how do we get out of here? I am not sure mija, but we are going to try.

I we both quickly got up and slowly started working our way to the door. We reached the door and my grandfather said let me stick my head out first, grandpa let me you have been through so much and besides, I am here to save you. What was I kidding I got kidnapped faster than my grandfather, but my grandfather being a great man that he is let me take the lead? I slowly poked my head out and there was no one in the hallways. Grandpa, where clear follow me I told him. I began to walk out, and I ran right into someone. Oof, I said I placed my hand on whatever I bumped into and I felt pecs, huh, I pushed off and my hand slowly went down and stopped on a rip abdomen. I quickly brought my hand back and said I am so sorry when I looked up, I noticed who it was. Lucifer quickly covered my mouth and pulled me back into the same room I just tried to sneak out of. My grandfather was ready to attack him, but I quickly raised my hand and motion no. Lucifer what are you doing here? Who else is going bring the angels down here to fight? He smiled that devilish, extremely attractive smile. I see where Mammon get that smile from. Lucifer, we need to go to Mammon, Luna is crazy, and I think she will kill him. Oh, my dear do not underestimate my son. I taught him everything I know, well mostly everything. So, what do we do? My grandfather quickly said we cannot trust him. Why not? Lucifer looks at my grandfather and says Yes, why not? And do not give me that he is the devil crap, or that will enrage me.

His eyes got bright red and I knew exactly what that meant, okay calm down lucifer. I am just having some fun, calm down grandpa I am the one who brought the angels here, maybe not in the best way, but they are here that is all that matters. I am not sure what he meant by that, but I have a feeling we will find out. Grandpa right now he is all we have if he were not on our side, he would have chained us back up. I grabbed my grandfather's hands and I said I know you do not trust any of them, but grandpa please trust me, he is not bad he is here to help us I believe that. My grandfather stood quiet for a little almost wanting to keep arguing but he did not he kissed me on my forehead and said okay, but I want you to know I am trusting you. Okay Lucifer lead the way, I grabbed his hand and whispered I am trusting you do not let me down. Sweet, sweet girl his eyes changed into this vibrant blue; trust is all I need. He smiled this flirty smile and started to walk down a hall. That was a little creepy stair. Suddenly you could hear Mammon screaming, he sounds as if he is in excruciating pain. Then we heard her laugh, oh my son such weakness you have. This desire to love comes from your father, YAMARIES! He screamed; I was ready to run to him but lucifer stopped me and knobbed his head side to side telling me no. My heart broke, he was in a lot of pain, she is gone, and I killed her because she is your weakness, I heard Luna telling Mammon. She lied to him why does she want him to become king so bad, I asked myself. Lucifer looked at me and my grandfather and whispered you two stay here, she is strong I will deal with her. Believe me this will not end well for one of us, she is strong her mother is one of the eldest demons and she is a pure breed demon which means both of her parents are demons, very powerful demons. Okay that scared me a little bit, okay I trust you go save him before the angels get here. His eyes changed color to bright red, he smiled and said lets party, and walked towards her. Could he be anymore corny.

Luna darling long time no see. Wow, I said to myself he got jokes. How has it been down here in your new world, I hope full of misery and disappointment with a touch of despair. Lucifer, you are disgusting excuse for a king, oh but Luna dear I was not so disgusting when you gave me two beautiful children. Oh well my, my, he looked over at Mammon and said there is one of my children. The boy with daddy issues, but where is my girl with mommy issues. Luna did not look impressed, Lucifer that is none of your business and for your information our daughter has daddy issues as well. The kids only remember you ripping them from my arms, well that is to bad lucifer said shall we tell them why you where ripped out of their precious little hands. Well, I do not think we have to anymore you have already shown him your other side. He might have already gotten an idea. What do you want lucifer? Oh, Luna dear to kill you of course, to finish what I could not do all those millennium ago. Lucifer drew his sword from a wave of his hand and this gold and very shiny sword appeared from midair. So, you stole Michaels sword? Luna laughed she raised her hand and this black smokey almost human spine looking sword appeared. She stood her stand s and lucifer smiled and said oh and by the way the angels are coming, they think you and your tricky friends stole Michaels sword. Please do not ask how my brothers are not very smart, but they are fierce just listen to their trumpets. I closed my eyes because for a second, I forgot that they where coming. I could hear the beautiful sounds of the war trumpet; they are close I told myself. Your treacheries demon Luna hollered; how dare you bring them to my domain. Nevertheless, they will die on those high horses they rode in, by my demons. Welcome to m world baby, now let see who dies first, she is brutal I told myself she does seem stronger than I thought. Luna took the first charge at lucifer, when their swords collated it was the most ear wrenching noise ever. I felt the room shake and a gust of wind, that is insane, the force and strength of those two seem evenly matched. I must find a way to free mammon, while she is distracted. I cannot let lucifer do all the work, I quickly maneuver through the rumble, Luna and Lucifer were creating. As I am getting closer to Mammon I stopped and got distracted by the different colors that emerged from every blow the swords made. It was very hypnotizing, the fought as if they were dancing in a ballet. It was unbelievably beautiful to watch, shh... I heard, I looked over towards my grandfather and he is waving me to keep going. Thank god he snapped me out of it. I quickly got myself together and got to mammon. Mammon are you okay? That was a dumb question I told myself. Why do we always ask that question when clearly, he is not. Yamaries? Yes, mammon it is me. Oh, you are alive, I am so glad to see you. Mammon there is not time for reunion stuff we must free you and get you out of here. NO! I am going to stay here with mom and become king of hell. No, mammon listen you cannot, your father is alive, and he is going to kill her, you are going to be free. No, he will not win my mother is not to be trusted, she has something extra up her sleeves. Huh, what do you mean? Suddenly mammon stopped speaking and dropped his head. Oh no! I quickly began to unhook him from those chains, and he fell to the ground. Oh, I am sorry, I did not mean to drop you like that, I leaned in to hold him an get him back up, once I touched him mammon's eyes changed to pure black, it was scary to see. His eyes made him look as if he had no love, no emotions, no care only pure evil and nothing else. Mammon I said softly, he glared at me with those eyes,

I felt a chill go down my spine. Mammon, it is Yamaries, your Yamaries remember? Mammon got up looked down at me and said no, you are not Luna killed you, I was weak and thought you where real. You are not and now I shall go and take my place as king. Mammon waived his hand and a bright red and black sword appeared, I had to get out of the way, I thought he was going to stomp on me. He really did think I was dead.

What has she done to him, he quickly charged at lucifer and I yelled Lucifer look out! He quickly drew another sword and swatted at Mammon. Son, you must fight do not let her take control, Luna quickly looked over at me with this nasty look and said you nasty little sphinx, you let go of my secret weapon way to early. No matter I was not going to need him, Lucifer is far to weak and old to fight with a higher demon like me. Now little human I am going to show you what it is like to be part of our world. She began to charge at me, as she was coming closer with the sword, I brought out my hands to cover my face and I heard a cling and a burst of air. I opened my eyes and realized that there was another sword blocking Lunas, no mother your battle is with me. Yvi! I yelled she pushed her mother back. Yvi, you have no idea how happy I am to see you. Yvi smiled and said you getting soft on me? I smiled at her, lets keep focus my mom and her minions are nothing to fool with. Draw a sword and get ready their coming. Luna looked up her eyes turned this dark purple; she placed her hand around her mouth and made this horrific sound almost mimicking the angel's trumpets sound but badly. Everyone stopped once the floor shook, what the hell was that? I asked myself. This is it Yamaries Yvi yelled, you must summon a sword, you want to be with my brother you must fight like you belong with him, fight as our queen.

Call it intuition or call it I seen to many hero movies, but I felt this burst of energy, I brought up my hand and said come forth my sword. I was so excited I began to feel this tingly feeling going up my arm and into my fingers. I looked at my hand and eww, there was a spider on my finger. I quickly shook my hand and made sure it did not bite me. Of course, that would happen to me and o n top of that embarrassment no sword. Okay I guess it does not work that way; how I can summon a sword. Is there like a spell or a certain way to move my hand, shoot we did not cover this on fighting 101. I started to look around to see if I could use anything else as a weapon but could not find anything except throwing rocks like a true cavewoman. I began to see eyes starting to appear around us, oh crap their here Lunas little demons ready to kill us all. They began to launch out and attack Yvi and Lucifer as they fought, I did not notice the one that was charging towards me. I was focus on looking for a weapon when I heard my grandfather yell out Yamaries look out! I quickly looked at him and everything went in slow motion, I seen him pointing at something and he was pointing vigorously. I turned towards the direction he was pointing at and noticed this small hair yellow eyed creature coming towards me. I quickly turned my body towards the creature and went to go block as the creature came flying at me. I cannot really remember how I did it, but I summoned a sword, the most beautiful sword. The sword was blue a beautiful shiny blue with a red glow. the sword was magnificent, I swung my hand and the creature burned. Wow! I am awesome, I began running towards all the creatures swing my sword like I knew what I was doing. I probably looked like a mad woman; I can say this whatever I was doing was working because I was killing those demons. As I am trying to kill lower demons I looked over at Mammon and Lucifer, and Mammon is fighting with so much hatred the darkness in those black eyes. I am not sure what Lucifer did to hurt him so much but whatever it is it shows, The way he swung that sword was like he was telling a story, I could feel his pain with each swing. I am so sorry you hurt my love, I was distracted and did not notice little demon coming at me, he was so fast that I did not get enough time to block his attack. I fell to the ground and hit the back of my head on a rock, I think I was knocked out for a minute or two, when I came to the little demon were all over Yvi and her father. I tried to sit up but got dizzy and felt a sharp sting in the back of my head. I reached back there where the stinging was at and felt a lump. Ouch, ugh I looked at my hand and surprise, surprise there was blood. I did not have the strength or the time to be thinking about why I am bleeding. I got up and almost feel again but on to a pillar that was next to me. I closed my eyes and said Yamaries hurry up they need your help. I placed my hand over my face and wiped what I hoped was sweat, I opened my eyes and was focus on killing those creatures. I summoned my sword flawlessly and charged. I ran towards Yvi first to help her; I am glad you are up I was beginning to wonder. Wonder what? I asked her as we were both swinging our swords. How can these little creatures be the ones to take out the great Yamaries? Ha-ha very funny, she laughed and that was the first I heard her laugh and seen her smile. You need to smile more often Yvi you have a beautiful smile. Be quite human, do not get friendly, once we got the creatures off Yvi we both turned to help Lucifer. We swung our swords and took little breathes before each blow. It felt good to have the last stroke of my sword and kill a demon.

Well, well Ladies you defiantly are one of a pair. You fight great together, cut it out dad, we need to figure out where mom and Mammon went. Umm, guys where are my grandfather? I cannot believe I let him out of my sight. Umm, Yamaries Yvi said Luna took him. She walked over to him took a big smell and took off. Mammon let out this blood hurdling howl and all these creatures came out of every nook and crack there is. I really thought we were not going to make it; I cannot believe I did this to you all of you all. I never meant to place all of us in danger, Yamaries Lucifer said this was your destiny. You were meant to come down here and set things straight, it is written a half breed would come and restore order. So, you see it is not your fault. Now it could have been less bumpy on the way were you not so hasty, really, he went there made me feel good and then boom drop. Okay, I will admit I rushed into stuff, but I was scared to miss my grandfather or worse get here to late. I was already a year behind on saving him. Yamaries you need to stop taking things and doing them on your own. You are not alone anymore you have us and we will win together. Now let us go save your grandfather and my son. Dad I do not mean to rain on your parade, but mom moved so fast I did not even get a chance to see at least what direction she went. Oh, honey I do, before our little fight got shall I say barbaric, I placed a little device in your mom's skin, it made her bleed she thought I scratched her. I have learned one or two things from the humans. Okay and how are we going to see where she is at, well he pulled a cell phone out of his pocket. Do you know how to work that I asked him, just because I am old my dear dies not mean I cannot learn new tricks, believe me I pick up the times very quickly. I am so sorry, no need Yamaries let us leave the apologies for a later time. Now ladies it looks like she has gone that way, he pointed at an opening that was dark and creepy. Of course, she would go that way, alright then I said out loud shall we go in or just stare at it. Lucifer laughed, such in a rush Yamaries, always in a rush, what does that suppose to mean? Like I told you always in a rush, no plan. Do not add obstacles Yamaries, we want to get to them quickly and quietly, I wanted to snap back, but I took one look at Yvi and everything started flashing back. Everything that happened was my fault Mammon getting drugged, punched out, everything he did, he did for me because of me. Oh, wow everything he has done rushed, okay what is the plan? Good sweet Yamaries goo, I am going to need you two to follow my lead, when I tell you to do something and only when I say you will make a move. Okay I had a lot to say about that, but he knows what he is doing, and I trust him. Okay let us do this, Yamaries he said I am going to need you to hold every emotion and instincts that makes you do impulsive things because in order for this to work everything must go as I say. Really? He is going to beat that horse when it is down, yes Lucifer I hear you loud and clear nothing without your okay. Good let us go, we began to walk over to the dark opening with Lucifer in the lead, the minute I lost site of the opening everything in the cave shined blue it was beautiful, so calming and relaxing. Girls Lucifer whispered, keep your eyes open and do not get to relax this cave has a spell. It will put you to sleep and you will never wake up. I quickly started to try and snap myself out of it, but it was getting hard to, for a moment I think I feel asleep, I felt very cold and I could not move like if I was constricted. It smelled different like a hospital, I tried to open my eyes and there was a bright light it hurt so I closed my eyes again. Yamaries I heard, Yamaries are you okay? It was Yvi, I either woke up or snapped out of whatever that was. I am okay I will not fall asleep I promise I am going to fight until the very end. That is the kind of fight I want to hear, I smiled and kept walking, each step it got harder and harder to stay awake. Every time with a flash of the bright light, and I jolt back to reality, that is so strange why is it affecting me this way.

It felt like we were walking for a while, just when I was about to complain we saw a purple light. I know those colors I said to myself, mid-way Lucifer raised his hand for us to stop. He looked at us placed a finger over his mouth letting us know to stay quite and pointed at his ear to listen. We stood quiet; we could faintly hear Luna speaking. I closed my eyes to try and hear carefully what she was saying. You are fragile little boy, get over her loss and be a man. It is time to kill your father and become king with me as your second helping you rule hell like it should be. Leave me alone mother, I need to be alone. Poor Mammon sounded broken, the love of my life is hurting, and I am stuck here listening to his mother torturing him. STOP THAT! She yelled; it irritates me to know you are soft like your father. Believe me, I wanted your sister because she is stronger than you will ever be but unfortunately women are not allowed to rule which should be disband since men are weak. Lucky for your father he had me by his side, he was so strong I the beginning and then he got soft once I made the mistake of giving him you and your sister. Lord, she talks to much I told myself, I was so concentrated on Luna's discussion with Mammon I did not noticed that Lucifer was staring at me. I finally snapped out of my listening trans and mouth out What? All he did was smile. He is so weird, I told myself, he whispered to me listen harder, what in the world is that suppose to mean, okay I whispered back. I closed my eyes and tried to listen, the only thing I could hear was Luna still torturing Mammon. I tried to tune her out because she was starting to upset me. Off in the distance I could hear the trumpets, faintly but they were there. Oh man how did I forget about the angels, they are going to turn this all around, I just know it. I looked at lucifer and smiled let him know I new exactly what he was talking about. Okay ladies now listen carefully he whispered, once the angels burst through that will be over chance to get Mammon and get you guys somewhere safe. We will handle the rest. No lucifer I whispered, I want to be there when they kill her, she has caused a lot of pain to Mammon and it will give me great pleasure to watch her die. Lucifer smiled, I smiled back not knowing what exactly that meant, but I am hoping that means yes, I could stay and watch. It felt heart breaking to stand there and listen to that awful monster just torturing mammon and I was not able to do something, that crazy chick went from torturing him with words to adding physical torture as well. I looked over at Lucifer, giving him the when are they coming look. He whispered patience; I was about to say something when this loud crash came in. Lucifer Hollard at me and Yvi NOW! I began to run as fast as I could towards him. I need to hold him and care for him, let him know that I was right there and not going anywhere. As I was running towards mammon, I could not help but take a glance of the angels, they were magnificent, they look like something from a movie. So perfect and beautiful, one thing I did noticed was they were all guys. Gorgeous guys but guys, nonetheless. I finally reached Mammon who was hanging from his hands, bleeding not really moving. Mammon I said it is me Yamaries you must get up, Yvi got to him just a couple seconds after me and was trying to get him to move and speak as well. Yvi I said try to get him untied maybe he will respond. She began working on the knots and I continued to speak to him. Mammon please get up, open your eyes, show me those blue eyes please, my patient was starting to wear out, it was turning into panic. Yvi I said sounding hysterical, he is not responding Yvi please I cannot lose him do something. Yvi finally got him loose, and he fell in my arms, wow, he is heavy. He smelled so go even though he was all bloody he smelled like something sweet and he was all mine. Yvi came down to our level and said big brother you need to open your eyes; we are here to save you. I began to cry and as dramatic as it sounds, he began to moan. I looked down and said Yvi he is moaning. She smiled and said yes, I know my brother is a fighter. We both began to laugh, and Mammon said please let this be true, Do I hear my Yamaries voice and my dear sister laughing with each other. Ha, ha I mocked, you have jokes. I knew my crazy mother was lying to me, she could never destroy someone like you. My sweet Yamaries, stop talking Mammon I must find your father we have to take you to safety. I lifted my head and seen this great battle happening right in front of me. When did those demons get here? How long have they been there? There were knives clashing as they smashed against one another. Magic spells being cast and things appearing in mid-air. The whole thing was very mesmerizing, which in all this I searched for Lucifer and I quickly found him when he summoned one of his knives. Can you believe he was fighting Luna? Her purple glowing knife banging against Lucifer's red glowing knife was something to see. There I Hollard at Yvi, your father is there, I did not want to react so hastily, so I looked at Yvi and said how do we get his attention/ I am not sure she said. Like this, Mammon said, he got up and let out the biggest roar. The angels all covered their ears and the demons ducked in fear. MOTHER! It is time to pay for your sins, he said with this powerful voice. His eyes shined this black, blue color. His wings were out, and they were this beautiful white and blue. He began to rise, so focused on his mother. Luna looked very afraid; Lucifer was mouthing something I really could not understand. Luna Morning star you wanted a king, now you shall have a king. Mammon raised his hand up in the air and said "Necrom I summon thee" Lighting sparked, and this blacked spine with red shine appeared, it looked horrifying. Is that human spine I asked myself? Mammon took off after his mother, the anger filled the room, Lucifer kept looking at me yelling something. I wish I learned how to lip read, because I have no idea what he was trying to say. I looked up at Yvi hoping she could help me but when I turned around Yvi was standing right behind me and shoved a knife right at my stomach. Silence, complete and utter silence, I could not believe it, she betrayed me. I was in shock, I coughed, and blood dripped from my mouth. Why/ was the only thing I managed to say. Yamaries, you know this is what was supposed to happen, she pulled the knife out and stabbed me again. I fell to the ground in the pool of my own blood, she leaned in close to my face and said you ruined our family, I was starting to fade in and out. Our families name is now garbage because of you. My eyes closed and I felt this cold air, is this how a spirit feels when they disappear. I slowly began to open my eyes and there was a bright light, I closed my eyes quickly and held them closed. I am so sorry, I said Yvi I am sorry. I tried to move to hold my wound, but I could not move. Oh no, my body is completely numb, I thought to myself. Mammon! I yelled, help me, as blood kept dripping from my mouth. He will never love you Yamaries, he cannot you hurt this family to much. I opened my eyes again and I could see Yvi's outline but not her face with the bright light behind her. Yvi I did not mean for all of this to happen, I was just trying to… I coughed, Yamaries? Who is Yvi? I was lost huh, what? I was so confused, it sounded like Yvi asking that question. Yvi? I said why are you asking… I felt like I was fading. Shhh, Yamaries, wait I know that voice, aunty? What is going on? I opened my eyes, and everything was blurry. I began to shift but I really could not move, I blinked a couple of times and everything was getting into focus. Yvi so called outline was my aunt, I looked around and I was in a small room with white walls, a small desk and chair, and the bed I was laying in. I got scared, aunty how did I get here? Where is Mammon? Yvi? And Lucifer? Yamaries what are you talking about? Aunty where am i? I began to cry, why can I not move? Oh god aunty I have been stabbed by Yvi she betrayed me. Yamaries, stop it. Why are you acting weird aunty, you now? Yamaries listen to me now do not speak, you are in the hospital, I looked down at myself and I had this jacket tied on that normally are part of the Mentally ill. Aunty, where am I? please aunty let me out, LET ME OUT! I yelled and growled at my aunt. These two men in white clothes came running in and held me down as my aunt got up quickly, began to cry and ran out. They gave me a shot that stung, and I slowly feel to sleep. Blackness, I did not dream that night, it was all black. I was awakening the next day when I heard someone say inmate 147621 Gonzalez, Yamaries time to get up and eat breakfast. A tray was shoved in through a whole in the door and then closed again. I really could not rap my head in around it, but I tried to move, and I noticed I was free. I sat up slowly because I was still a little foggy from the medication, they gave me yesterday. I placed my hands on my head and said to myself what happened to me. I got up and walked slowly towards the tray, I got startled when I heard some say finally you are awake and alert. I will see you at noon for our session, I looked throw the whole and noticed a man in a suit. Do you understand? He raised his voice, yes sir, I said, good he replied. I was so afraid, I grabbed my tray and walked over to the desk, I laid the tray down and noticed I had a wrist band on that had the numbers 147621 and my name Gonzalez, Yamaries. I sat there and just looked at my breakfast tray, I did not eat anything one was because I was not hungry but two is because I have no idea what or who served me this food. I could not risk it, what happened? How did I get here? I asked this question repeatedly in my head. I was trying to piece together the events that happened while I was in hell and how did I get back on earth? I sat like this until noon, when a man in the white uniform came to my door and said inmate 147621 it is time for your session. I got up from my chair and he said walk over to the door and place your hand in the whole please. I walked over to the door and placed my hand in the whole, he placed handcuffs on me, and it hit me. I was in jail why am I in jail? Sir, I said why am I in jail? What is going on? Inmate please step back so we could open the door, no you must tell me why you placed these handcuffs on me? Why am I in jail? Calm down he yelled, you need to calm down or we will have to give you another sedative. I got myself together quickly and just got quiet, good he said, and he opened the door. Two other men came into the room and grabbed me and walked me out of the room, we walked by other rooms and I could not help but look in. Some of those people where talking to the wall, others where yelling and some just sat there looking lost. I was the scariest place I have ever been in and I went to hell. We finally got to the hall where there was this big door you could tell this is where the man with the suit worked in, they knocked on the door and he said come on in. They pushed the door open and I slowly walked in, the men closed the door behind me and the man in the suit said please Yamaries have a seat, I swear the walk to the seat felt like a death sentence. I got to the chair and sat down slowly, I am glad that you are alert and coherent, I have been waiting a long time to talk to you. Umm, sir, I am sorry, but I do not understand what you mean, you do not remember? He said that like if I was lying. No sir remembers what? Well this is a surprise, well he continued what do you know? I was… and then I stopped, if I tell him I went to hell to save my grandfathers soul he will really keep me here. I am not dumb so I will not answer that question. Yes, Yamaries continue, he said sounding extremely interested. I am sorry I cannot remember anything; do you know who you are? Yes sir, my name is Yamaries Gonzalez. Good Yamaries good, what else do you remember? I went to go live with my grandparents after my father died. Yes, perfect, and then, well sir that is it, I did not want to keep going because I was going to go into the whole possession and demons, and I did not want that. Are you sure, Yamaries there is nothing else you would like to share? I had to think quickly because I did not like the way he was staring at me like if he knew I was lying. Oh, my I am so sorry sir I almost forgot my aunt, what about your aunt Yamaries? She is getting married to the chief of police, he is such a sweet man. Is that all? Yes, sir after that everything goes blank, he is such a pushy man. I must take the upper hand, sir if you could please explain to me what is going on, it would really help.

This is incredible, okay Yamaries I will help you remember some stuff, but you will have to remember the rest on your own. I will give you a piece of information, Yamaries you are here because you murder someone. My heart dropped, excuse me sir, I could never hurt anyone. I could barely kill a bee without feeling bad afterwards there has been mistake. I began to hyper ventilate, I please there must be some mistake, tell me you are lying, YOU ARE A LIAR! I growled. The two white men came in and quickly grabbed me and gave me a sedative. I slowly fell asleep, when I awoke, I was back in that small room in the bed. Once again, I felt foggy and now, I was irritated, why can

I not remember anything? When did I come back, did I fight Zozo, did Luna die? I was going crazy just thinking about it, I looked around the room to try and distract me from thinking so much and I noticed I had a small window all the way on the top in my room where I defiantly could not look out from. I got up and walked back and forth trying to remember, it got dark and suddenly a voice said you could never get rid of me. The voice sounded like me but eviler, excuse me? How are you? Ha-ha you do not remember me? Now that hurts, it laughed. How are you? I will not ask again? Come take a look in the window, I am right there. I walked slowly towards my door to look at the window, when I looked at the window it was me staring back at me but the me when I was merged with mammon. Hiya Yamaries remember me? OMG, what? I looked down at my hands and I looked normal, I looked back up and she was staring at me with a smile. Stop looking everywhere I am you and you are me, except I am a better version I think of you. What do you want? I began to cry, ugh, you cry to much. You really cannot remember what happen and I appeared. No, I do not, well this is going to be fun. Look deep Yamaries search you will find it; everything will come to play. Everyone needs to stop playing and tell me what is going on, fine Yamaries hold on, he-he it is going to be a bumpy ride. It felt like a jolt and I landed on the floor my eyes rolled to the back of my head and flashes began to appear. It starts back when I first arrived at my grandparent's house, then it flashed to when my grandfather was going on the fishing trip. A flash happened and I was in the woods where my grandfather's body was found but it was dark, and he was still alive with the other gentlemen's, another flash and I have a bloody knife and everyone was dead, I looked down and I was over my grandfather's body. Oh my god, no I did not, then a flash again and I was in the living room where my aunt noticed that my feet where dirty. Flash, I was standing in my grandmothers' room over her bloody dead body and my hand had the knife. No, please stop no, I did not do this, Flash, I was standing by my aunt's fiancé who was bleeding and holding out his hand telling me to stop, now I heard my voice, No Zozo will never listen to a human, for I am a god, the king of evil. Welcome to my world, Aww, no I did not do this, this is not me.

So you see Yamaries you are a murder and you enjoyed every single minute of it, but do not worry dear I will help you get through your life sentence here in death row for the criminally insane. I could not bear it anymore the pain, I really did kill my grandparent's and my aunt's fiancé, I am a monster. I got up and thought to myself I made everything up, I never went to hell. There is no such thing as Mammon and Yvi and Loard, I made that up. Who am I? I looked a t the wall and looked at my desk, I walked over to the other end of the wall looked at the door and I ran as fast as I could and ran right into the wall as hard as I could. Everything went black, Yamaries, are you going to get up now? I know that smell, I thought to myself. Come on sleepy head we must start our day off. It was him Mammon, the love of my life, I opened my eyes and I was in his room on the bed and he was next to me. He smiled and said welcome to hell where your worse nightmare can come true. I am a monster; I belong here, and I will take my reign as the queen of hell.